WARRICK'S HOPE

THE DRAGON RUBY SERIES

LEILANI LOVE

Copyright 2017 Leilani Schweitzer

This work is licensed under a Creative Commons Attribution-Noncommercial-No Derivative Works 3.0 Unported License.

Attribution — You must attribute the work in the manner specified by the author or licensor (but not in any way that suggests that they endorse you or your use of the work).

Noncommercial — You may not use this work for commercial purposes.

No Derivative Works — You may not alter, transform, or build upon this work.

Inquiries about additional permissions should be directed to:
leilanilovebooks@gmail.com

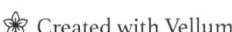 Created with Vellum

OTHER BOOKS BY LEILANI LOVE

Violca's Dragon

The King's Fire

Violca's Vow

Kassandra's Wolf

Warrick's Hope

DEDICATION

This book is dedicated to my boys.
They are always proud of me and encourage me in both good and bad days.
My family and my friends who I love like family.
I also want to give a special thanks to all those who have left me a review
and sent me a message. Those always come at the perfect time.
You guys are the best and I am very blessed.

PROLOGUE

Warrick knew this was a dream the moment it began. A memory he had dreamed about so often he began to wonder how much was true and how much was just his mind filling in the blanks. His parents had dragged him to the neighboring town where the Blue Mountain wolf pack lived. He didn't want to go. Why couldn't his dad understand he had a life too? He had plans that day to go on a date with a girl from school to get burgers and shakes.

After he met the pack leaders, his parents had dismissed him. Annoyed he had to ruin his plans he walked aimlessly around the small town. It was quaint and you could tell that despite being small, the town was definitely flourishing.

He ate lunch alone at a small diner. Warrick was envious that his twin brother, Gabriel, wasn't forced to come. Since he wouldn't be inheriting the pack, his parents had let him stay home. Before they had left this morning, Gabriel had joked that he would take Sue out to lunch for him. Warrick had attacked him and they'd started wrestling. His father had burst into the room, pulling them apart and yelling that an Alpha does not attack his pack members over a silly girl. His father didn't understand. He never understood. As far as his father was concerned, no female really mattered except for a wolf's true mate and Warrick should just ignore all of them and wait for her. But he was fifteen and the idea of not being able to date who he wanted frustrated him.

Warrick wondered how much longer he was going to have to wait for his parents so he could leave. Hopefully he'd still have time to take Sue out. He had already wandered all the downtown area, and visited most of the shops. As he stood outside on the corner of the street deciding what to do next he caught wind of an intoxicating scent that caused his body to instantly tense. It was the faint smell of flowers with a hint of something earthy he couldn't quite identify. It called to the animal in him making it his only priority, to find who that scent belonged to.

His eyes scanned the crowd as a gentle breeze coming from the south caught his attention. There it was. Her scent again. He turned to find her. As he began to walk that way through the crowd of people he heard a woman yelling. The crowd parted and he was surprised to see a little girl no more than four years old running straight toward him. She was laughing as she ran. Her little legs were surprisingly fast as the sun shone on her honey blonde hair.

Warrick was surprised to realize that the scent was coming from the little blonde-haired hellion. Stunned, she ran straight at him and jumped into his arms, which instinctively reached out to catch her. Her amber eyes lit up with mischief as she patted both of his cheeks with sticky fingers. "Mine." She declared before giving him a big smile.

"Yours," Warrick whispered unable to help himself from smiling back at her.

She laughed as he shifted her in his arms to hold her more comfortably and was surprised when she put her head on his shoulder. When Warrick looked away he saw an older woman running toward them holding the hand of a little boy who looked to be the same age as the girl. The two looked very different except for the same amber eyes and matching mischievous smiles.

When the woman stood before him Warrick llooked her over. She didn't smell anything like the two kids. She looked to be about fifty with salt and pepper hair and fine lines around her blue eyes. Even though she looked fifty, he knew she was also a wolf and that her aging process would be slow like his. "Hope, you know better than to run off. What would your mother say?"

Hope, was a perfect name for the little girl. He watched as Hope looked at him, giving him a playful look before she looked down and gave the little boy a big smile before saying, "Mine."

The little boy smiled back. His dark wavy hair framed his face and Warrick watched as they exchanged a secret look before looking at him. The little boy seemed oddly familiar. It took him a moment to realize why he recognized the boy, he was almost the spitting the image of his father, the pack alpha he had met earlier.

The happy moment seemed to be etched in his mind forever and he lived it over in his dreams. The moment he found her. He wished the dream would end there but this is where it always changed. Flames. So many flames and the little girl he held in his arms was suddenly in front of him before running off. Warrick screamed as he chased her through the fire and straight up to her house. The flames were so big and high surrounding the house but when he heard a scream he knew he had to go in. Warrick had to try to save them. As his mate her family was his family.

As soon as he entered the burning house, his lungs filled with smoke so he held his arm over his face to protect his lungs from the heated air. He did his best to follow the screams upstairs until he ended up in front of a closed door. The sound of someone coughing reached him so he kicked down the door and found a woman on the floor. Once he reached her, he picked her up, but before he could get out he heard the distinct sound of floorboards breaking. He didn't have time to respond before the entire floor collapsed out from under him.

The feel of flames licking his skin. The smell of flesh burning as he tried to get his bearings. He had to find Hope. He tried to scream her name, but smoke filled his lungs and he began coughing.

Warrick's eyes started to water and he fell to his knees. The flames singed his skin. The pain so intense he knew he wouldn't last. Trying one last time he screamed, "Hope!"

When his eyes opened he suddenly found himself staring into a pair of amber eyes that were bright with unshed tears. Could she really be here? Was this just another dream? Before he could come up with any answers he felt a sharp prick in his arm and his world went black.

THERE WAS A MOMENT, before he passed out, when Warrick's cobalt blue eyes met hers and she thought he might have recognized her. It was the first time that he had awoken since they rescued him from his brother's clutches. Jared, the young dragon-shifting guard, was careful when picking him up, trying hard not to jostle him, but with the amount of bones Warrick had broken there was no good way to move him.

"What did you give him?" Hope asked the doctor who had been called in to help.

"I gave him some more morphine. I need him to stay still so that the bones we just set have time to heal before he begins to move," the doctor said, his voice soft and patient.

Hope looked up at the doctor who was checking Warrick's heart rate. He was an older human whom Viktor had called in. Viktor was the King of the Dragons and he had assured her that Dr. Raine had often been called in to help his family and he could be trusted.

"I'm going to set up a drip to keep him under. Between his natural healing ability and Violca's constant healing touch I don't think we'll need to keep him drugged too long. I just want to make sure they're set right," Dr. Raine announced, giving her a sympathetic smile.

Hope smiled at him. She hadn't really noticed much when they'd arrived at Viktor's house, her focus had been on Warrick. She was happy when she started noticing Warrick's heartbeat growing stronger and how he started getting a little color in his cheeks.

When they'd first arrived and Violca tried to shut her out of his room, Hope thought that she would have to fight with the witch to be allowed access. Instead, she was allowed into the room and watched while Violca touched Warrick gently. The air itself changed when Violca had touched him, it felt almost electric and the scent of magic had filled the air. It wasn't oppressive like the town Gabriel was controlling. Instead, she felt drawn to the witch. When her sisters walked in and touched Warrick that feeling grew, along with the strength of her magic.

"He's going to be out for a while. You should eat and get a nap. Let's make you some food, then I can stay and watch him while you get some rest," Dr. Raine said while patting the hand Hope had resting on Warrick's bed.

Hope took a deep breath, she wanted to tell the doctor no but her stomach gave a distinct rumble that made him smile. She pictured him as a grandfather. His hair completely silver, slightly thinning, wire rimmed glasses and a small belly. She let him lead her from the room looking back one more time at Warrick, who was sleeping soundly.

He was still thin but the scar that ran down the side of his face was no longer puckered, swollen, and looking angry. His body was covered with smaller scars but the one down his face looked the most vicious. It started on the right side of his face, just under his eye and ended close to his jaw. Dr. Raine had pointed out that less than an inch higher and he probably would have lost his eye.

As they left the room and Hope let the doctor lead her down the flight of stairs, she began to feel guilty. She half listened as he told her that Viktor had made sure that there was plenty of food prepared and she was welcome to go to the kitchen and make herself at home. For the first time, she realized exactly how late it was. The house was quiet with only a few small nightlights illuminating the hall, guiding them to the kitchen.

"When he wakes his body is going to be hungry but I don't think he's eaten a full meal in a while. We will need to make sure he only eats a little bit at time. If he's like every other male patient I've had he'll complain at first. Don't let him win," Dr. Raine finished telling her before opening the fridge. "Now let's get you fed so you're strong enough to help take care of him."

1

TWO MONTHS LATER

Today was the day he would be moving out of Viktor's spare bedroom and into a house that both packs had rebuilt for him and Hope to live in. When the two had first imprinted on each other the packs thought that it would unite two of the strongest packs along the East Coast. With everything that had happened the packs were a shadow of their former selves and now the packs looked at Hope and Warrick as a sign that their lives were going to be turning around.

Damien, the Blue Mountain alpha, would be staying with his dragon-shifter mate Kassandra. Damien's house would be built last and would reside right next to his. For the first time, two packs would live together in the same town.

Thanks to Dr. Raine and Violca's healing touch, Warrick was left with only a few scars and a slight limp. The doctor had informed him that after so many breaks he was surprised how well they had healed. He had, however, given most of the credit to Violca, who was a descendant of the original Earth Witch and had the gift of healing. She was the oldest of five sisters all of whom had their own gifts. Over the last two months, he had gotten to know them all quite well.

A soft tap on the open bedroom door pulled Warrick from his

thoughts and he looked over to find Damien standing in the doorway. "You ready to go?" Damien asked.

Warrick grabbed the small bag at the foot of his bed. "One of the perks of traveling light I guess. Not a whole lot to pack when it's time to go," Warrick said. He had arrived with nothing more than the clothes on his back. Luckily, he was close to the same size as Damien who had given him some clothes to wear.

Damien was Hope's twin brother and had spent the last two months helping move both packs from West Virginia to Colorado. Damien had given them a choice to go out and make it on their own, or move and make a fresh start. A few of Gabriel's loyal guards had chosen to go off on their own but the rest had quickly volunteered to move and stay together.

Warrick was still surprised by how much had changed. With Damien mating with a dragon-shifter they had formed an alliance. When Viktor, King of the Dragons, had offered to help them rebuild a small town near his, Damien had taken the offer. Warrick of course could choose to move his pack elsewhere but there was strength in numbers, and he also thought it would be the best way to protect his people.

They drove from Viktor's to his new house in silence. Damien seeming to understand that Warrick had a lot on his mind. The town wasn't finished rebuilding yet. The first house they built was for him and Hope. Warrick didn't feel totally comfortable moving in with her. He still felt awkward and with his limp and several scars that would never fully heal he felt out of place when he was with her. Hope was breathtaking. She'd grown up to be even more beautiful than he had ever imagined.

Warrick wondered how Hope was feeling about everything. For over forty years she had believed Warrick had been the one who had killed her parents and tried to kill both her and her brother to gain control of both packs. In the last two months, however, they had learned that it was actually his twin brother using black magic to trick them and that Hope and Damien's mother was in fact alive. Their mother had arranged for Lazzaro, the Vampire King, to save them before the attempt on their lives was made. She managed to also get letters to Lazzaro that he was to deliver to Damien and Hope, but only after Warrick was rescued. He knew that they both desperately wanted to find and rescue their mother but in those letters, she told them that they needed to focus on rebuilding both packs; that they would find strength in numbers, and that she was okay. Her power as a seer protected her and she would be with them before the birth of her first grandchild.

That last line was in both their letters and neither Hope nor Damien knew which of the two she was referring to. Damien seemed like the obvious choice since he was already living comfortably with his mate, Kassandra. Warrick felt guilty that Hope was tied to him. Their moving in together was a decision that had been suggested by Aithne, the Dragon Queen, as a way to show the packs that things were indeed changing.

After Hope had agreed, Warrick conceded as well but asked to make sure she had her own room. Warrick didn't have any belongings so he suggested that the master bedroom be hers and he would take one of the extra rooms. Damien had given him a questioning look at the suggestion but didn't argue.

When they pulled into their new town, Wolfbourne, Warrick found himself impressed with the amount of rebuilding they had done. The buildings that had been abandoned for decades now looked like they were almost ready to re-open. Damien had broken them into groups. They had been focusing on rebuilding some of the homes that just needed light work first, then a few of the shops so the town could start bringing in money and support itself. Besides rebuilding, the pack was learning to fight and defend itself by training alongside the dragons. Warrick had been given clearance to begin training last week and looked forward to joining the men.

As they rounded the corner to the road that led to his new house Warrick was surprised to see how many people had lined the streets. He swallowed hard and waved to the people as they passed. "They have been planning this party for weeks," Damien said as he drove slowly up the road, careful of the kids that were running around.

Warrick nodded keeping his eyes focused out the window. Kassandra had told him that they were going to be having a feast in their honor. He had tried to convince her that it was not necessary. Kassandra smiled politely and told him that both packs were celebrating his recovery and the completion of many homes to come.

The crowd parted enough for the car to drive slowly up the road and Warrick's heart stopped when he saw his new residence at the end of the road. It was a two-story colonial looking structure complete with a matching white picket fence. This would be his new home, and standing on the front porch was the woman he'd been dreaming about for the last forty years.

"Are you ready?" Damien asked Warrick, pulling him back to the present.

"Is she okay with this?" Warrick asked, realizing that asking her twin brother might not be the best thing. Unfortunately, Warrick really had no one else to talk to.

Warrick turned to look at Damien who was staring at his sister on the porch. "For years I thought the Fates had doomed me and Hope to live alone. If I learned anything from our childhood it was that they could kiss my ass." Damien shot him an apologetic glance. "I still don't know what their plans are, but for once I can admit I was totally wrong. You and my sister got a raw deal, and now you two need to figure out how you want to move forward."

With that, Damien got out of the car leaving Warrick no choice but follow. As he stepped from the car the crowd let out a loud cheer. The number of people that had showed up to celebrate them moving into their home surprised Warrick. As he followed Damien through the fence to join Hope and Kassandra they were stopped constantly by the pack members who thanked them for the new chance.

Warrick stood at the bottom of the stairs and the crowd quieted, watching him and Hope. She had dressed in a white summer dress. Her honey blonde hair blowing in the soft breeze and amber eyes shining brightly. For a moment, he thought she was going to cry but she blinked back the tears with a smile saying, "Welcome home, Warrick."

2

Hope greeted Warrick and waited perfectly still for him to join her. Everyone was silent and she saw a quick look of unease cross Warrick's face before he finally took his first step up the stairs. The crowd erupted in loud cheers upon Warrick's approach.

As she looked upon him, her breath caught in her throat. Warrick had shaved, but she knew from visiting him that he preferred a little stubble on his cheeks and kept his hair very clean and around his shoulders. She was thankful for the roar of the crowd because it drowned out the thumping of her rapid heartbeat. When he got to the top of the stairs, Warrick leaned down and gave her a chaste kiss on the cheek before turning and facing the crowd. Along with Kassandra and Damien, they stood together presenting a united front, smiles plastered on their faces as they greeted their packs.

Kassandra had arranged for a barbecue to take place in the backyard. The four of them were expected to greet the oldest of each family on the porch while the rest went into the back. Hope knew the importance of this as she smiled politely at the first elder to greet her.

"We're so glad to see the two of you together," one of the elder females told her as she took her hand. "You and your family bring hope to us all," she continued as she beamed up at Hope.

"With everyone's hard work this town will be growing in no time. Thank you for blessing us with your visit," Hope said, surprised when the elder woman gave her a motherly hug.

The guests all made a huge point of stressing how happy they were to finally see Warrick and her together, and telling Damien what a strong match he'd made with Kassandra. Kassandra stood between Hope and Damien. This was the first time that a wolf shifter had mated with a dragon shifter. With everything that had happened Damien wanted to make sure that everyone accepted her. So far, there had been no incidents but Damien often worried about his mate.

"Looks like it's time we join everyone in back," Damien said after he talked to the last elder. Hope watched as he laced his fingers with Kassandra's and felt a stab of envy at how close the two had become.

"Are you ready?" Warrick asked looking down at her.

When she nodded, Warrick offered her his arm and she took it. The two of them following behind the other couple as they walked around the wraparound porch. Hope had to admit Kassandra had done a wonderful job of setting up the backyard. It was set up to be casual and Kassandra had even removed the backyard portion of the fence in order to use the property of the unfinished neighboring yards down to the open woods behind them.

As Hope and Kassandra took their seats, Damien and Warrick got up to get some food leaving them alone. "Warrick appears to be healing well," Kassandra said giving her an encouraging look.

Hope nodded glancing over at Warrick. Hope still remembered that moment they'd found him chained to a table in a basement. For so long she thought he had betrayed her and her family, never knowing his brother had set the whole thing up and was using black magic to trick them all. Hope still felt the sharp sting of guilt realizing that for all those years she had been wrong and could have saved him. "The doctor finally gave him the okay to start training and help out with the building," Hope said before meeting Kassandra's knowing green eyes. "I think he would have started the moment he woke up if he could've found a way around Viktor or Damien."

Kassandra laughed and Hope couldn't help but smile. She liked her brother's mate. Kassandra, affectionately called Kat because of the unique slant of her sea-green eyes, had long, light blonde hair and a curvy, muscular figure. Hope had heard the men talk in awe about how Kassandra had easily taken down a wolf guard when they'd rescued the packs from Gabriel, Warrick's twin brother.

Kassandra was a dragon shifter, or a weredragon as they were often called. Much to Damien's dismay Kassandra was one of the Dragon Elite guards who'd met him while on a mission for her king. Hope still laughed thinking about how Kassandra had drugged her brother the first day they met.

"Men make horrible patients," Kassandra said with a teasing grin. "I've a feeling if your brother ever gets sick I'll have to tie him to a bed and stuff a gag in his mouth."

Hope laughed so loud the tables closest to them turned to look, which made her laugh harder.

"Should I ask what you two find so funny?" Damien asked as he put a plate down in front of Kassandra.

Kassandra gave him an innocent smile before saying "You know, girl stuff."

Damien looked past them to Warrick who was setting their plates down and snorted. "You know that means they were talking about us."

Warrick smiled a little as he took his seat before glancing at Hope. "Better to make her laugh than cry, right?"

"True," Damien said before kissing Kassandra on the cheek. Hope noticed him whisper in Kassandra's ear which caused her to blush. This made Hope look away, feeling as if she had been watching something private.

Hope looked down at her plate. She was surprised to see a nice filet mignon wrapped in bacon with a baked potato and corn on the cob. She knew Viktor was funding the barbecue; he was also helping to support the town until they could get back on their feet. Hope had no idea how they were ever going to pay him back. Gabriel had taken all the money that the pack had earned over the last forty years. Aithne, Viktor's mate, was using Gabriel's laptop and was trying to track down what he had done with the pack money. When she glanced at Warrick out of the corner of her eye, she noticed a slight flush on his cheek as he ate his food.

The rest of the night passed by too quickly for Hope and before she knew it, she was standing on the porch, waving goodbye to the guests with Warrick. Once the last guest had left, Damien kissed Hope on the cheek whispering in her ear, "If you want you can stay with me and Kassandra for a bit longer."

Hope blushed knowing that Warrick's increased hearing had probably allowed him to hear Damien. She shook her head whispering, "I'll be fine."

Damien gave her one last look and Hope turned to give Kassandra a hug goodbye. Kassandra returned the hug with a smile then turned to hug Warrick. "If you guys need anything, call," Kassandra said before taking Damien's hand. "Call us in the morning when you're both awake. We can look over schedules and I can bring over donuts and coffee."

"Thank you," Warrick said giving her a smile. Both of them stood on the porch watching as they left.

Hope felt a moment of panic as she watched the red taillights of Damien's truck leave down the main street. Clearing her throat, she looked up at Warrick and for a moment she thought he looked as panicked as she felt.

"You know you don't have to stay if you don't want to. No one would know if you chose to stay with your brother tonight," Warrick said turning to look at her.

Hope felt like someone had punched her in the gut. She debated for a moment about getting in her car and taking her brother up on his offer. Lost in her own thought she almost missed how he stood in front of her. His body so tense she wondered if pushed, would he fall.

"My place is here with you," Hope said simply while walking past him and into the house.

It took a few minutes for him to follow her, but she waited patiently. When he finally stepped into the living room she noticed him looking around and realized it was the first time he had seen the house. When Hope had asked him questions about furniture he didn't really seem to care much so she tried to pick something neutral.

Hope had chosen mostly masculine colors and furniture she hoped he would find comfortable. The couches and chairs were a tan color and the wall had a built-in bookcase that also housed the big screen TV.

"Here let me give you the grand tour," Hope said leading him from the living room toward the kitchen.

"I turned the smaller downstairs bedroom into a small office. The other I made into a guest room," Hope said pointing to the two rooms at the end of the hall opposite the kitchen. She then led him into the kitchen which opened into the dining room and kitchen nook.

In the morning, this room would be filled with morning light. Hope had talked to Damien and he was going to put in a bench seat for her at the window. She loved to wake up early, sip coffee and read a book and that spot looked perfect.

"My mother used to love to make cookies every Saturday. They were always gone by Monday," Warrick said as he looked around. "She would've loved this kitchen."

Hope, for the first time since everyone had left, saw a hint of a smile on his lips. "I remember your mom's cookies, when you two came to visit. Your mother was very nice."

Warrick nodded and she felt a sense of grief coming from him. When she was little she was too consumed with her own grief to really understand that the fire she thought had killed both her parents had also killed his. Gabriel, in his quest for power, had not only killed her parents but theirs too, and then turned his back on his twin brother. Hope wondered if she would ever be able to understand what would drive someone to do that.

"My mother really liked you. I still remember her face when I showed up holding you in my arms that first day," Warrick said, a smile tugging at his lips.

Hope blushed. She was so young when she'd met him but she remembered when his scent had hit her. She had taken off running and remembered hearing the sound of her nanny yelling as she followed. Damien seemed to understand and actually helped slow down the nanny so she could reach Warrick.

He cleared his throat and she felt her cheeks heat up more as her eyes met his. "Ready to see the upstairs?"

"Sure," he replied following her as she walked up the stairs.

There were three bedrooms upstairs. The first one was set up as another guest bedroom. The second one was the room she had set up for him at his request. Hope had wanted to give him the master bedroom but he had refused, stating that he would prefer a smaller room. His room had a door that connected with the bathroom.

"I didn't know what colors you liked so I asked Damien to help pick something out," Hope said as they stepped into his room.

The room was the second largest and was big enough for a queen size bed. The furniture was made of cherry oak and she had picked a dark blue for the sheets. The room they had found him in had been so dark Hope had wanted to make sure this room was brighter, adding touches of color and a big window. After Viktor mentioned seeing Warrick read several books on history, Hope had gone to the store and bought him a bookshelf. She found books on different historical topics along with some fictional books by authors she knew her brother had liked.

"Thank you," Warrick said as he looked around.

"My room is across the hall. If you ever need anything..." Hope said her voice trailing off. It didn't feel right, him being in this room.

"I'll be fine," Warrick said as he went to the window to look outside.

"Okay, I'm going to take a shower and get ready for bed."

"Good night," Warrick said giving her a polite smile.

Hope nodded before walking out of his room to go to hers. This should be easier, he was her mate and she was his. Destined by the

Fates to be together forever. If it wasn't for Gabriel, by now they would have probably been married and had several grandkids running around to babysit. Instead, they were strangers. Hope had no idea how they were going to get over the past. Her only thought was that they had a second chance and she wanted to take it.

After a long hot shower, Hope curled up in her bed wondering how Warrick was doing across the hall. Kassandra had gone shopping with her when she'd bought the furniture for the room.

"King size bed, huh?" Kassandra had teased her when she had picked it out. "I take it you don't plan on sleeping alone for too long."

Hope had blushed as she touched the four-poster bed. "You know, as a kid I used to imagine that somehow it was a mistake and that somehow everything would work itself out. As an adult, I never..."

Kassandra touched her arm. "It'll work out. You two both just need to get to know each other." With that, Kassandra looped her arms in hers as she signaled for the salesperson to come and check them out. "Until then the two of us can get drinks whenever you want and we can talk about how stupid men are."

Like his room, the furniture was cherry oak, but instead of blue she'd chosen dark forest greens. She bought enough furniture so that if and when he was ready he could easily move his stuff in. As she settled into the bed, she heard his door open and his footsteps as he walked down the hall to the stairs. Hope resisted the urge to follow him and see what he was doing. Instead, she closed her eyes and worked on slowing her breathing and quieting her mind so she could fall asleep.

3

This dream was different from the others. Warrick stood in the doorway and saw Hope walking toward him, her belly big and round with their child. A warm inviting smile on her lips as she walked over to him. As he stood in front of her, he put his hand on her belly. Then, while cupping her cheek, he dove in for a deep kiss.

"Are you feeling okay?" he asked.

A small laugh escaped her as she rubbed her belly. "Yeah, your son just decided he needed more room and we're working out a deal about my lungs being in his way."

He chuckled, putting his hand over hers. "Be nice to your mom little man. She's the only one you get."

She excused herself, walking toward the kitchen and the dream slowly shifted. The walls and the floor slowly started going up in flames that grew as she walked away from him. Warrick was calling and running after her, determined to save her but the hallway just seemed to continue to get longer.

Before he could reach her, his brother Gabriel stood before him. He was holding Hope in his arms with a large knife pointed at her belly. A sadistic smile on his face as he stood glaring at Warrick. Before everything had happened the two were identical. Now Warrick's body was riddled with scars, including the long one on his cheek and he would forever walk with a small limp.

"I told you, the two of you would never be together big brother," Gabriel said as he ran the knife along her belly. "You couldn't save her when she was younger and there's no way you can save her now."

"No!" Warrick yelled as he lunged for his brother.

As his eyes flew open, he felt two soft hands on his arm and Hope's muffled voice as she said his name. Warrick's hands were wrapped around Hope's small neck. Stunned, he immediately released her and a rush of guilt flooded his emotions. He sat up helpless as she struggled to regain her breath.

"Hope, I'm so sorry," Warrick said as he started to reach for her. When she pulled back a little he felt even worse knowing he must have scared her. "Hope I..."

"It's okay," Hope said, her voice scratchy as she rubbed her neck. "I should've been careful. I knew you were having a bad dream."

Every word Hope said got a little louder and he knew she was starting to catch her breath. "I shouldn't be here. I..."

Hope put her hand on him and shook her head, "Warrick this is your home. It was an accident. I'm okay." When he gave her a nervous look and she gave him a reassuring one in return. "I promise."

They were both quiet and as his eyes adjusted to the dark he looked her over. Hope was in a white tank top; her nipples had hardened and were poking through the material. The shirt went to her waist and he couldn't help but notice the curve of her shapely thigh as she sat on the edge of his bed.

"I'm sorry I woke you," he finally managed to say as he looked away from her. His voice huskier than before.

"Can I ask what the nightmare was about?"

Warrick shook his head not sure what she would think about him dreaming about her pregnant. "Just Gabriel," he muttered before finally looking up at her. "You should go back to bed. I'm okay now."

He watched Hope bite her lip looking indecisive before she finally agreed. "Okay, try and get some sleep."

Her voice was barely a whisper and Warrick watched as she stood up. Her shirt did nothing to hide her lower body from his gaze and the white panties she wore teased him. When she turned, he had to bite back a moan because they were cut to reveal the bottom half of her shapely ass. Round and pert, he couldn't take his eyes off it as she walked toward the door.

When she stopped and turned, Warrick forced his eyes to look up at her face and he felt his cheeks heat up at having been caught staring at her. "Sweet dreams Warrick," Hope said, closing the door to his bedroom before he could reply.

He adjusted himself as he leaned back in the bed. For the first time his mind filled with thoughts of what it would be like to meet and imprint on Hope now instead of when they were kids. With no scars, his body totally healthy, what it would be like to simply meet her and seduce her.

Hope had a beautiful soul. He had watched her tonight after they had finished eating. She and Kassandra had gone around talking to people and playing with the kids. He had laughed when she had what Damien had told him was a foam dart gun. Hope and Kassandra had chased the kids around shooting them and laughing when the kids had finally turned and started shooting her.

She was sweet and kind, all Warrick could think was that she deserved to have someone that wasn't broken. Not haunted by nightmares or constantly having to look over his shoulder to keep her safe. Gabriel had always threatened to kill Hope if Warrick ever broke free. Several times over the year Warrick had wanted to just give up and die, but every time he came close, Gabriel had reminded him that if he died Hope would be the one to take his place.

"Do you think she'll scream?" Gabriel would ask him as he ran the knife along his side. "I've never had a virgin. Poor Hope, she has to be in her thirties now and as long as you're alive her wolf will never let her sleep with another man. But if you die..."

"If you touch her, I'll kill you," Warrick would threaten while struggling against the chains.

Gabriel had chuckled before sliding the knife into his side. "You couldn't save her before big brother. I should've been born first. You've always been weak."

Warrick stayed alive just to keep Hope from the hell he had been living in. Gabriel had told him one night after drinking too much that he had tricked everyone into believing he was him. Using his blood magic and black magic to trick both packs. It crushed him to think that she believed he had killed her parents and had tried to kill her.

But she was safe. That was all that mattered. He would suffer for all eternity so long as Hope was safe. Now that the two were together, Warrick worried that Gabriel would come through on his threats and come after Hope. Damien and Viktor were training the packs to fight and defend themselves and Viktor had a few of his dragon guards help patrol their town, promising to help keep them all safe from Gabriel in case he decided to get his revenge.

With no sign of Gabriel in the past two months, Warrick wondered where his brother might have gone. He didn't know much about the witches that would visit Gabriel. They were the complete opposite of the Earth witches that resided with the dragons.

Those witches had been beautiful on the outside but the first time one of them had touched him, his skin crawled and his wolf had growled wanting to be far from her. She had smiled, a cold calculating smile before talking to the others. "This one is strong," she purred. "He'll be perfect."

At the time, he didn't know what they had meant but after the first time they cut him and collected his blood to cast their first spell, he understood. They were going to use Warrick and his imprinting on Hope to make them think Gabriel was him. The smell of sulfur had curled in his nose and the more they came around to cast their spells the more he felt like he was covered in a sticky film. He had been surrounded by it so long that when he awoke and for the first time felt clean, he thought for sure he had finally died.

Warrick tried his best to push his wayward thoughts aside and fall back to sleep. As his eyes finally closed he heard his brother's distinct voice in his head, "Do you really think you can keep her safe? I'll always be stronger."

4

After tossing and turning the rest of the night, Hope went downstairs as soon as the first rays of sunshine started peeking into her room. Throwing back the covers, she grabbed a short robe at the foot of the bed. The red silk robe barely covered her ass and for a moment, she debated about putting on a pair of sweat pants. She wanted a relationship with Warrick. One where he slept with her at night. Hope had a feeling if she pressed too hard he would run but she saw him looking at her last night and felt, at the very least, that he was interested in what he saw. Maybe she could use that to her advantage. The man might resist, but if his wolf was anything like hers, it just wanted to be with its mate.

Downstairs she started the coffee. Not much for eating the second she got out of bed she made herself a cup with plenty of sugar and creamer before sitting at the dining room table. Hope reached up and touched her throat thinking about the events of last night.

She had woken up to the sound of him screaming her name. Hope had run into his room thinking that someone was attacking him. She had felt his pain and when he screamed, "No!" she couldn't help but touch him. She had been unprepared when his hand had wrapped around her neck and squeezed hard enough that she could barely say his name to wake him.

The sound of the back-door opening caused Hope to jump. Getting up, she walked to the kitchen, surprised to see Warrick standing there. Used to being alone she didn't even think to check and see if he was in the house when she woke.

"You're awake," Warrick said as she walked into the kitchen.

"So are you," Hope said, as she looked him over. Warrick flushed slightly and she wondered how long he had been awake and what he had been up to.

"Would you like a cup of coffee?" she asked needing to break the awkwardness.

"Yes, please," Warrick replied before saying, "Black."

With a nod she made him a cup. When she'd put her robe on she had hoped to entice him but since he was already dressed and had been outside she felt a little awkward. When she turned to give him his coffee she noticed he had been watching her and that his blue eyes had darkened in just the slightest way. Hope cleared her throat as she handed him the cup. "I should get dressed. Damien will probably be here sooner rather than later, even if I don't text him."

Warrick reached for the cup and for the briefest moment his fingers brushed hers and she felt a shock of awareness. Having imprinted on Warrick at such a young age, she never had any interest in anyone else. When the girls in school would talk about boys and how their stomachs quivered in excitement, Hope would lie and say she had felt the same. But for the first time she felt that quivering sensation and a desire to lean into someone. Warrick's face had gone blank and she sighed. As Hope walked up the stairs she wondered if she was the only one who felt this way.

ONCE DAMIEN ARRIVED with Kassandra the two men went into the office to discuss pack business first. With both of their packs moving to the same town, Damien and Warrick were both determined to rebuild them to their former strength.

Kassandra, with a box of donuts in hand, had taken one look at Hope and offered her one. Choosing a chocolate donut, Hope curled up on the opposite side of the couch from Kassandra and sighed.

"Rough night?" Kassandra asked as she tucked her feet under her, her body turned so she could face Hope.

"I don't know what the Fates were thinking. We imprinted so long ago and so much has happened since then," Hope said. Hearing the pout in her voice, she took a bite of the chocolate goodness wondering how much chocolate she would need to eat to feel better.

Kassandra sat there with a smile on her face. "You know you're talking to the girl who drugged her mate the first time they met, right?"

Hope laughed. Her brother Damien's distress about meeting his mate followed by having her drug him made him so mad she felt it and rushed over thinking something had happened. "That was funny," Hope said, still laughing at the memory.

"I wish dragons recognized their mates by scent like you guys do. Would have made things a little easier with your brother," Kassandra said, shrugging her shoulders. "Neither one of you guys are responsible for Gabriel's greed. But you're both going to have to figure out how to put it behind you in order to be happy."

"I wish I knew how he felt," Hope said as she looked toward the office door.

"Have you thought about just seducing him?" Kassandra asked, a big smile on her face.

Hope blushed. She could feel how hot her cheeks were and by the grin on Kassandra's face she knew her friend was enjoying her discomfort. *Could she seduce him?* She was a virgin. *Would she even know how?*

"I don't even..." Hope started to say unable to meet Kassandra's gaze.

"You are a beautiful woman, Hope. The Fates have already decided you're his. He just needs a little push in the right direction,"

Kassandra said still grinning. "You don't have to be too aggressive, small touches here and there. Just be... overly friendly."

Before Hope could open her mouth to reply, the office door opened and Warrick and Damien came out. Both of them had a look of relief on their faces and Hope couldn't help but think at the least the two of them were getting along.

Damien came out and walked to Kassandra giving her a kiss. Hope looked away pretending not to hear how her brother told Kassandra he loved when she tasted like chocolate. A glance up at Warrick showed he felt just as uncomfortable.

"The barbeque was a success and I was telling Warrick that in a couple of days we should have several of the other homes ready for the families to start moving in," Damien said as he grabbed one of the donuts. Offering the box to Warrick, he took a seat in the chair closest to Kassandra.

"That's good," Hope said, feeling guilty for thinking about her own problems instead of the pack. "What can I do to help?" she asked looking between the two.

"There're a few women that are going to be cleaning up the homes, maybe you can just check and see what they need. They'll also need furniture. Could you work with the store and maybe come up with some items that could be delivered soon?" Damien suggested with a shrug. "The list of families and addresses of the homes are in the office."

Hope nodded and after a few more minutes they all got up to take care of things. Kassandra was helping set up all the kids in school while Damien and Warrick were both going to help finish up with the grocery store. That would be the town's first stream of income. After that they were going to take a group of men and train with the dragons.

After she finished getting ready, Hope walked to the door. She was surprised when Warrick grabbed her hand, stopping her. "Be careful today. Maybe have someone go with you to pick out the furniture."

Hope nodded giving him her best reassuring smile. "I'll see if one of the girls at the house wants to go."

Warrick nodded and for a moment she thought he forgot he was holding her hand when he suddenly dropped it and rubbed the back of his neck. He looked so vulnerable that Hope couldn't help herself and kissed him on the cheek goodbye.

"Have a good day, Warrick," Hope said before exiting quickly, not wanting to see his face.

Hope made her way to the homes on the list that Damien had given her before she left. Dressed in a pair of jeans and an old grey shirt she had pulled her hair back ready to get dirty by helping clean up the homes. The five houses were next to each other and she noticed that the one on the lefts front door was partially open. She walked up on the porch and quietly entered the house making her way into the living room to see if anyone was there. She followed the sound of laughter to find a group of women of all ages in the kitchen.

They all stopped when she entered the room. Hope smiled at each one. She had met them briefly last night. After meeting so many people over the last few days she felt bad she couldn't remember everyone's first name. The girl standing by the table seemed to be the leader of the group. Hope smiled brightly remembering her name was Sandra.

"Hi. I came to see what I could do to help?" Hope said feeling uncomfortable when no one spoke.

At that, the group instantly wwelcomed her, everyone telling her hello at once. Sandra came forward and surprised her with a hug. Sandra had long dark hair and brown eyes and if Hope had to guess, was probably in her thirties. "Thank you so much, we're just finishing up our coffee and trying to figure out which house we wanted to tackle first," Sandra said with an easy smile.

5

Warrick spent the day with the electrician trying to help wire the buildings. He wasn't able to do anything major on his own but was able to get him set up so things went smoothly and they were able to finish two of the four buildings. The grocery store and the gas station looked to be on track to open by the end of the month.

Viktor had offered to give them the money to get everything up and running but a wolf's pride ran deep, and instead they finally agreed on an interest free loan. The families that were interested in running the small businesses had submitted an application and Damien and Warrick were to pick families to be the individual owners, along with making suggestions for managers. Several of the wolves had found jobs in the surrounding towns with Viktor's recommendation. Warrick and Damien were hoping that they, as a community, could start supporting themselves by the end of the year and begin to pay back Viktor for all his help.

After spending the better part of his day with the electrician, Warrick drove to Viktor's to spend a few hours training. Warrick needed to get his strength back in order to protect Hope. He wanted to convince himself that the voice in his head was just his mind playing tricks on him but with him and Gabriel being twins, there was a chance Gabriel was talking to him through their connection.

As Warrick walked to the training grounds he heard Chase's voice say, "You need to keep an eye on your surroundings even during a fight. Just because there's one person there when you started the fight doesn't mean a second one isn't coming up behind you."

Warrick stepped around the corner just in time to see Chase grab one of the wolves from behind, holding him in place making him an easy target. Chase released the trainee before telling him to go back in line. "Some days you can do everything right, and nothing will go your way. Just remember always keep your head. The fastest way to lose a fight is to lose your temper. Keep your calm and remember your training."

With that Chase dismissed the class and Warrick watched as a mixture of dragons and wolves walked toward the barracks. While he had been recovering he'd eagerly watched the training sessions from his window, wanting to join them and stretch his muscles.

"Warrick, good to see you," Chase said a smile on his face. "Did you come for a private lesson?"

Warrick shook his hand in greeting, "Yeah, if you have the time. I tried to get here before you started training but we're almost finished wiring the second building and I couldn't get away."

Chase nodded taking a swig of his water. He was just a little shorter than Warrick, standing at about six feet tall with golden brown eyes that turned completely gold when his dragon came out. Warrick had only seen him change once, when his mate Violca was outside. Before climbing onto her mate's back she nuzzled the dragon's neck whispering to him. Since the town was nestled into a remote section of a mountain range the dragons were able to shift and fly as long as they stayed aware of how far they had gone. For that reason alone, the rangers kept strict accounts of when and where tourists were in the area.

"Sure, we could do some one-on-one. Since they pair up I don't get much of a workout," Chase said looking toward the house. "Just make sure you don't push yourself. Violca will skin me alive if I let you hurt yourself after all the work to get you up and walking."

Warrick laughed, nodded, and kicked off his shoes. After walking in on Warrick in the halls at night, doing what the doctors called physical therapy, when he thought everyone was asleep, Chase had decided to help him out. Warrick fully expected Chase to lecture him but he instead gave him a cocky grin before saying, "Violca says I'm the worst patient, but you might have me beat."

With that, he had helped him walk around for part of the evening, pushing him a little more every night. When the two of them were ready they circled each other. As Warrick looked for an opening he was surprised when Chase asked, "So how is it finally living with your mate?"

Warrick lowered his guard for a moment, not sure how to answer then he saw Chase throw a punch. He managed to duck just in time. The punch was so close he felt the wind brush his hair. Warrick used this position to land a punch to Chase's side. He took a step back and saw Chase curving his lips into a grin. "Funny, never heard the guys complain that you fight dirty."

Chase chuckled and the two of them circled each other again. "Not dirty, but I do believe in teaching people not to get distracted during a fight."

The two of them continued to spar. Every time Chase landed a hit or a combo he would take a moment to teach Warrick how to defend himself against such a move. When Warrick landed a combination, Chase praised him and then gave him a few ideas on how to follow up.

After an intense hour, the two stopped. Chase reached into one of the coolers and tossed him a water bottle. "Not bad, just make sure you keep that guard up and remember to follow through."

Warrick nodded taking a big swig of his water when he noticed Chase looking up the trail from the house. He smiled seeing Violca walking toward them. Violca was the oldest of the Earth witch sisters and was known for being protective over her patients.

"Warrick, I see you're obeying the doctor's orders not to push yourself," she said rolling her violet colored eyes, the sarcasm dripping from her voice. Her full lips tipped up in a smile as she gave her mate a disapproving look. "You better not have pushed him too hard."

Chase smiled, reaching out and pulling her into his arms. "Of course not," he said before giving her a quick kiss.

When Chase released her, Warrick couldn't help but notice the soft blush on her cheeks. Warrick and Chase put on their shoes and walked with her back up the hill. Warrick liked Violca. There was something calming about being in her presence. She was also brave. Hope had told him that it was Violca who had reached out to Lazzaro and began the truce between the dragons and the vampires after he had tried to kidnap her mate Chase.

Warrick had been surprised to hear that the Lazzaro had saved Damien and Hope when his brother Gabriel had tried to have them both killed. The relationship between wolves and vampires was an interesting one. At one point, vampires had tried to enslave them as guards during the day. When that didn't work, vampires tried to hire them. Some wolf clans had sold themselves easily while others looked down on the proposal.

"I am glad you're here Warrick. I wanted to check on you and extend an invitation to you and Hope for a small get together next month," Violca said as she walked with them up the hill.

"I'll have to check with Hope but I don't think it'll be a problem. I just don't know..." His voice trailed off. He realized he had no idea if she had any plans, nor did he know what she normally did.

Violca gave him a smile. "I'll text Hope and you the day and time and you can just let me know. I was also going to invite Lazzaro and a few other people. I wanted to keep it small."

Warrick nodded and when they got to the top of the hill he said goodbye to them both and headed back to his new home. Since he and Hope had imprinted on each other and were mates he realized that everyone seemed to assume that they were a couple. After all they both knew that the Fates had decided they would be together. Unfortunately for them things didn't go as planned.

Warrick listened to the music on the radio as he drove. He missed the songs from when he was younger, so Damien showed him where the oldies stations were. There were still a great many songs he had never heard of and he definitely preferred classic rock to the music Angyalka and Sari, the youngest two witch sisters, had introduced him to when they were showing him what he'd missed.

When he pulled up in the driveway he saw Hope was already home and felt a yearning for something he couldn't describe. He needed to take a shower, between sparring with Chase and helping the electrician, he felt dirty. There was something nice about being able to shower and clean himself up whenever he wanted. After getting out of the car, he used the side door entrance.

The delicious smell of food hit him as he walked in and his stomach grumbled in anticipation. When he entered the kitchen, he bit back a moan at seeing Hope bent over, her heart shaped ass up in the air. Warrick's hand itched to reach out and touch her, make sure this wasn't one of those dreams that had haunted him over the last few years.

Hope stood up, closing the oven. "I thought I heard you come in." She looked him over and smiled. "Looks like you had a busy day. Dinner will be done in about ten minutes if you want to go clean up."

Her smile was contagious and he smiled back at her. "It smells delicious. I promise to be back down before it's done."

She nodded at him and he felt like he was supposed to say something more. Not sure what that something was, he gave her a nod and headed upstairs. Determined to be done before dinner was finished, he resisted the urge to enjoy the feel of the hot water cascading over his body. Warrick closed his eyes as he rinsed his hair. The second he did, the image of Hope bent over played before him. For a moment he imagined what it would be like if she was fully his and he could reach out and touch her like he'd dreamt of so many times before.

6

As Hope lay in bed she thought about the events of the day. After getting a list of supplies, Sandra had volunteered to go with her to the store to pick up everything. Once those were dropped off, Hope had to admit Sandra had been helpful with ordering furniture for the families.

They picked up a quick lunch and Hope found herself opening up to Sandra when she asked about how Warrick was settling in. "It must be a little awkward for you two. I mean for a long time you thought he'd betrayed you and he was innocent all along," Sandra said a look of sympathy on her face.

"It's not ideal, but I think we can work it out. We just need a bit to get used to each other and things should fall into place," Hope replied. Even she heard the lack of conviction in her own words. Sandra had given her a look and patted her hand.

"Well if you ever need to talk I'm always around."

Hope smiled realizing that it was nice having someone to talk to who didn't know her from before. The rest of the afternoon had passed quickly and when she arrived home she felt better than when she'd left. Since Warrick wasn't home yet, Hope decided it would be nice for him to come home to a nice home cooked meal. He had seemed appreciative and had told her about his day but they still didn't have a lot to talk about yet, so most of the dinner was spent in an uncomfortable silence.

Warrick had cleaned the dishes insisting it was his job since she had cooked. Hope had smiled and thanked him. He went to bed early and Hope decided to read in bed since tomorrow was going to be another busy day. With everything ordered for tomorrow, she would help them clean the houses to make sure they were ready to be lived in when everything arrived.

As her eyes finally started to close she thought she heard something outside her room. She frowned in concentration letting her wolf come to the surface, using its hearing to see if she could figure out what the sound was. The house was quiet for a long moment and Hope began to scold herself for being so paranoid when she heard the sound again. Not quite making out the words, she knew they were coming from Warrick's room and she bit her lip while debating what to do.

Based on last night's adventure she would need to be careful but couldn't let him suffer through another nightmare. Hope left her room and slowly opened his door. The light from outside shone on his bared chest and she carefully approached the bed. Warrick moaned, his body sweaty as if he had been running. Hope wracked her brain thinking of the best way to sooth him.

After the fire, Hope used to have bad dreams all the time and her brother had often crawled into bed with her, brushing her hair back until she calmed down. Just him being there had always soothed her and she hoped that she could provide that same comfort for Warrick as she carefully crawled into bed with him.

He turned toward her in his sleep and she heard his moan of pain. Hope made a soothing, "shh" sound as she carefully brought her hand up to his cheek. Warrick leaned into her touch and she let out a breath saying a prayer of thanks that the move didn't seem to wake him. With a gentle touch, Hope, slowly stroked his hair.

After a few minutes, Warrick's body started to settle down. He was no longer crying out and instead had leaned into Hope. Turned towards him, she kept stroking his hair, looking down at his head lying against her chest. Very carefully she stroked her hand down the scar that ran the length of his cheek. When they'd first found him, out of all the scars he had, this one had looked the most angry.

Warrick's wolf was what had kept him alive all those long years. There was no way a human could have survived the torture he had endured. When he nuzzled her breast. She felt his breath through the thin material of the nightshirt she had slipped on. Her nipple hardened to a painful peak and Hope felt her body tighten in response.

They were strangers and her response to him was purely physical. A side effect of the imprinting that had taken place so many years ago. When she was younger she had tried dating. Hope had gone so far as to be kissed by a boy. The second his lips had touched hers, Hope almost lost control of her wolf and she pushed him off her.

The next day at school she heard the kids whispering, 'Hope, warm on the outside and ice cold on the inside.' Boys had even started placing bets on who could defrost her. Well at least until her brother had overheard. She had never been as mortified as when she found out he jumped those kids and had gotten expelled. That was when Lazzaro had decided to finish their education with tutors.

Hope had cried to Lazzaro about how unfair the world was and how she just wanted to kiss a boy. She grinned now thinking about how the big Vampire King everyone was afraid of had let her sit on his lap and just let her cry about how unfair and mean the Fates were. "Life is not fair," he told her after she'd finished crying. "Il mio piccolo lupo, but one day soon you will understand that if everything came easy, it wouldn't be worth it."

Il mio piccolo lupo meant my little wolf in Italian and had always made her feel safe when he called her that when she was young. As she looked down at Warrick she realized how good she had it. She always had her brother and Lazzaro but Warrick had no one. His twin brother had not only betrayed him but had seemed to take perverse pleasure in his torture. How could one come to terms with that?

Hope noticed how still he had become so she bent down and

kissed the top of his head vowing that he would never feel that way again. Not just because he was her mate but also because everyone deserved to have someone. No one should feel alone.

She brought her hand to her mouth and yawned. Warrick's nightmare had passed, so she decided it was a good time to go back to her own bed. As she started to roll away from him she felt his arm tighten around her waist holding her to him. Maybe a few more minutes wouldn't hurt, she thought as she adjusted herself on his bed. Closing her eyes as she continued to play with his hair, feeling safe and comfortable in his arms.

HOPE WASN'T sure what started this dream but she found herself wishing it didn't end anytime soon. This was not the first time she had dreamt of what it would be like to be kissed but she had to admit this was by far her favorite.

The warm lips brushed across her and her lips parted on a sigh. A low moan escaped her as his tongue slipped in. She wanted nothing more than to focus on that glorious tongue when she felt a hand slide up the bare skin of her stomach and cup her breast.

A part of her mind kept telling her something was different with this dream but she didn't want to focus on that. For years she had wondered what it would feel like to have someone touch her with desire. Her body shifted and she felt the tongue in her mouth stroke against hers, encouraging her to play. She obediently followed it into a mouth and dueled with it.

No wonder kissing was so popular. Her entire body tingled with awareness and she wanted to never wake up. The hand holding her breast squeezed gently and she let out a moan that sounded odd, even to her own ears. As she arched her back, her breast felt heavier and her nipples hardened as something rubbed against them. When they stiffened to painful peaks her eyes shot open. She let out a squeak, breaking the kiss when someone pinched it.

The sound echoed off the wall as Hope became aware that she

was not alone, nor was she dreaming that the hand on her breast stopped moving. It held her nipple between two fingers and she felt her face heat up at the realization that it was not just her heavy breathing that she was hearing. Slowly she opened her eyes and they locked onto Warrick's.

Neither one of them said a word and Hope realized that she had one leg draped over his and that something was lightly pressing against the juncture between her thighs. A blush spread on her cheeks as she realized exactly what it was.

She felt him slowly pull away and Hope bit her cheek to keep from whimpering at the loss of his touch. "I'm sorry, I didn't..." Warrick started to say as his eyes searched the room.

"No, it's my fault," Hope said adjusting her shirt before getting out of bed. "You were having a bad dream and I must've fallen asleep after you calmed down."

Warrick nodded and she was glad that the sun hadn't completely risen yet. If the heat on her face was any indication, she wouldn't be totally surprised if Warrick knew she was blushing. Hope glanced down at the blanket and found she was staring at the way the blanket was tenting below his waist.

"I'm sorry I keep waking you," Warrick finally said, breaking the silence.

Embarrassed Hope darted her eyes elsewhere, shaking her head. She wondered briefly if he meant from him crying out during his dream last night, or from kissing her awake just a few minutes ago. Even now her body craved his touch and she was a bit disappointed that they had stopped.

"Warrick..." she started to say before closing her mouth. She didn't want him to apologize for waking her up. She had always depended on others to chase away her nightmares and now for once she was providing that same care for someone else. "Don't apologize, please."

When he finally looked at her their eyes locked. She could tell he was fighting the urge to say something. Instead he nodded and she smiled back. "Well since we are both wide awake, I think I am going to make us some breakfast."

She went into her room to put on a pair of comfortable shorts and regain her composure before going downstairs. As she glanced in the mirror she wondered what he saw when he looked at her. Her nipples were still hard and pressed against the material of her shirt. Every time she moved, the soft fabric rubbed her sensitive skin and sent a small wave of pleasure right to her core. Hope blushed realizing that the material between her thighs was damp in response to his earlier kisses. Her body had been waiting for him for years. Based on the hard-on she'd felt and seen this morning he was responsive to her as well. Did he ache for her like she did for him?

7

When Hope left the room, Warrick leaned back in the bed. He'd dreamed of her so often that he wasn't even sure when he'd realized he was kissing her. Was she awake when it started? Did she kiss him first?

As he slid his hand up the soft skin of her stomach, he heard her sigh softly and he almost lost it completely. Not sure when he became aware that it wasn't a dream, he knew the exact moment she became fully awake. That little squeak of surprise brought him back to reality fast. He shouldn't have tried to seduce her without her permission.

Warrick rubbed the back of his neck as he heard Hope slip from her room to head downstairs. She'd looked breathtaking when her eyes finally met his. Her hair across his pillow, her lips swollen from their kisses. The mental image of her caused his already hard cock to kick in protest at not taking his mate. He got out of bed with a groan to dress and join her downstairs.

Today he was supposed to help the electrician finish the wiring in the morning before painting the outside of the houses so the families could start moving in. The busy work of rebuilding the town felt good. It was also a chance for him to meet members from both pack.

Eventually the two packs might split apart but for now they needed to rebuild.

Dressed in a shirt and jeans, he headed downstairs. When he walked into the kitchen Hope had her back to him and was pouring two cups of coffee. He took his black but had noticed she preferred flavored creamers and sugar.

His senses aware of everything about her, he could smell the hint of desire still on the air. When she turned to put her creamer back in the fridge her amber eyes met his and he saw a slight blush on her cheeks. When she finished putting the creamer away he took a step toward her. "I am sorry about this morning. I shouldn't have."

"It's okay," Hope said cutting him off. "I didn't mean to fall asleep in your bed."

Hope turned away from him as he closed the space between them but as he took that last step she looked over her shoulder and their eyes locked. He reached up and pushed a stray hair back behind her ear. "You have every right to fall asleep in my bed. I feel like I should apologize. You haven't received a good night's sleep since I moved in."

He watched as the pulse in her neck picked up speed. The smell of her desire thickened in the air. His wolf was aware of it, aware of her, and it itched beneath the surface. His canine teeth pulsed wanting to finally mark her as his. He started to lean forward on instinct wanting to put his lips to the column of her neck, which was calling to him.

When his eyes finally met hers, he noticed how they had darkened and her lips were parted whether in invitation or to tell him to go he wasn't sure. Giving in to the temptation to kiss her was the easiest thing he had ever done and he bent down to capture her lips with his.

For a split second she was stiff under him. He started to pull back when he heard her low moan as her hand came up and slipped around his neck, pulling him closer. Her lips parted and he felt her tongue tentatively brush against his lips. Warrick growled low in the back of his throat as he opened his mouth allowing her tongue entry.

Warrick wrapped an arm around her waist pulling her close. She started to lean into him, her tongue gliding against his. A hard knock on the door caused them both to jump apart. There was something satisfying about seeing Hope breathing as hard as he was.

"Was your brother coming over early?" Warrick asked looking at the clock.

Hope shook her head glancing down at her clothes.

"I'll get the door." Warrick volunteered. She smiled brightly at him before heading upstairs. Taking a deep breath, he went to answer the door feeling conflicted about the interruption. He shouldn't have kissed her but his body was so aware of hers after waking up with her in his arms, he couldn't help himself.

When he opened the door, he was surprised to see a woman he didn't know holding a pink box and a container of coffee cups. She looked vaguely familiar but he couldn't remember her name. Her long dark hair was pulled back in a ponytail and her brown eyes widened in surprise, before she gave him a tentative smile. "Hi. My name is Sandra," she said looking a little uncomfortable. "I'm working with Hope today and thought I would bring some coffee and breakfast before we get started."

Warrick noticed how uncomfortable she looked and tried to give her a reassuring smile. "Of course, please come in."

As he led her to the kitchen area, he couldn't help but notice that she kept fidgeting and her eyes darted around the place. She was dressed in a pair of faded jeans and a t-shirt. Hope had mentioned that they had almost finished cleaning one of the homes.

Sandra opened the box and smiled at him. "I didn't know what kind of donuts you guys liked so I grabbed a few different ones."

"Thank you," Warrick said as he looked into the box. Not wanting to hurt her feelings he grabbed one of the glazed ones. When he took a bite she gave him a big smile. Not really sure what to say, he was happy to hear the sound of Hope coming down the stairs.

"Sandra, good morning," Hope said as she walked in, her eyes lighting up when she noticed the box of donuts on the counter. "Oh donuts!"

Sandra laughed picking up the box offering them to her. "I hope I didn't show up too early but just in case, I thought I would bring a treat."

Hope shook her head, looking up at Warrick and giving him a smile. "Sandra's helping me make sure we have everything the families need before they start to move into their new homes. She's been great at making sure I haven't forgotten anything."

Sandra shrugged. "Anything I can do to help."

Warrick sipped his coffee, watching the two girls talk as he leaned against one of the counters. He noticed Hope smiled often. There was something about her that put people at ease. The few times they had been out among others he noticed that people were drawn to her like a moth to a flame when she was near. He doubted he was any different.

Sandra, he thought was nice but something made him uncomfortable around her. Warrick was sure whatever the problem, it was with him and not her. For forty years, he had only seen his brother and the witches that came in to drain his blood to cast spells. The feeling of unease could just be because he had met so many people in the past few months and he wasn't quite used to it.

After Hope had finished her coffee and donut she got up and looked at her watch. "If we leave now we should arrive in town just as the stores are about to open and we can order the rest of the stuff on our list. We'll be back in time to help finish cleaning that first house."

Sandra nodded, grabbing one of the extra cups of coffee and giving him a polite smile. "It was nice to meet you, Warrick."

"You too," Warrick said returning her smile.

Hope came up to him and leaned close enough to brush her lips against his. "Will you be home before dinner?" she asked, surprising him.

"Yeah, I just have to help the electrician. Once we finish a few of the stores we're going to work on the houses that are just waiting on wiring."

When she looked up and smiled at him he felt his chest swell with pride. The look in her eyes reminded him of the one that his mother would give his father when she thought he'd done something amazing. He now understood why his father always puffed up afterward. There was something wonderful about having someone look at you like you'd just hung the moon.

Warrick watched as the two of them walked to the door. Sandra, the last out the door turned and gave him a smile. "Don't worry Warrick. I'll have her back early."

8

The next few weeks passed mostly the same way. Hope often found herself crawling into Warrick's bed after he fell asleep in order to help with the nightmares. Some nights she managed to crawl back into her bed before he woke up, other nights she awoke to feel his hand roaming her body. Those mornings Hope felt a wave of frustration when he became fully awake and stopped.

This morning was no different. Hope moaned softly, her back arching into his touch as he cupped her breast. Her hips were tucked into his and she could feel his hard cock pressed against her ass. Each time his fingers tugged at her breast she felt her core contract. She bit her lip not wanting to moan and risk waking him up.

When he pinched her nipple, her hips bucked against Warrick's and she heard him moan as his cock slid between her ass cheeks. She could feel when he woke up because his hand stopped. She bit her lip to keep from swearing out loud. She had heard her brother Damien make jokes about blue balls and how bad they hurt. Either he'd exaggerated or Warrick was in constant pain. Something she was obviously willing to help him fix.

"Hope," Warrick whispered, his breath on the back of her neck causing a shudder to run up her spine.

Unable to help herself she tilted her head, offering her neck in a sign of submission. Hope's wolf needed him to claim her. Based on the way his body tightened behind her, for a moment, she felt like he might finally sink his teeth into her neck and claim her.

The tension grew until finally Hope turned, rolling carefully to her back to look up at him. His face was tight, like he was clenching his jaw, but the look in his eyes told her he was the big bad wolf and if she wasn't careful he might just eat her. Her hand came up and traced his jaw. "Good morning Warrick."

His eyes closed, as he nuzzled her hand with his cheek. It was rare that he didn't jump out of his bed the moment he woke up. Kassandra had told her to seduce him, make the first move.

"Please kiss me Warrick." The words were spoken so softly, not even loud enough to be called a whisper.

He heard her. Warrick opened his eyes and they locked onto hers. The look so intense she felt her breath catch. She slid her hand from his jaw up to his hair.

"Are you sure?" he asked his voice laced with a tension.

With just a little bit of pressure she pulled his face down to hers. When she could feel his breath on her lips she whispered, "Please."

Warrick brushed his lips against hers. So soft she almost thought she imagined it. She could feel his body tight against hers. Hope arched her body against his, parting her lips. When he moaned she felt a shiver of desire and power. There was something oddly powerful, knowing that he wasn't as immune to her as he liked to pretend.

His lips captured hers and she moaned into the kiss. Warrick's tongue traced the seam of her lips. A soft gasp escaped her and when her lips parted she felt his tongue slide in. Her tongue came out and tentatively touched his. That feeling of power surged through her and she felt herself grow bolder. When his tongue withdrew she followed with hers.

The kiss grew in intensity until Hope found herself breathless and clutching at him. When he started to pull away a growl escaped her and again, she followed. She felt him chuckle as one of his hands slid up along her side, under her shirt, brushing her breast. The growl turned into a moan and she felt his lips curve in a smile.

"I've dreamt of what it would be like to hold you in my arms, Hope. You were always the light to my dark."

Warrick's words pulled at her heart. She slowly opened her eyes to find him watching her. Hope reached up and traced his tight jaw with a fingertip. "I dreamt of you, too. I never understood them until after we found you. I wish I'd understood them earlier. I would've found you sooner."

Hope watched a shadow cross his face and wondered what he was thinking. She could feel him pull away when she mentioned finding him earlier. She wanted to ask him about what his brother did to him but knew that he was more closed off than her brother.

"Your brother should be arriving soon. We're finishing the outside paint on two more houses so the families can move in," Warrick said before he started to pull away.

Hope sighed nodding. *That wall he put between them came back quickly* she thought. Her body was tight with need. She shouldn't have laughed so hard at her brother's frustration when she found him trashing the bar after his mate had drugged him and left. Hope knew her brother wouldn't laugh at her but she could see his stupid little grin now.

"I'm going to take a shower," Hope said as she walked out of his room. "Nice, cold shower," she mumbled as she stepped into the hall.

When the cold water hit her body, Hope gasped and quickly turned the hot on, adjusting the water to a much more favorable temperature. She honestly didn't know what was worse, the fact that the wolves could smell that they hadn't been together or that she smelled of sexual frustration.

She had heard the women talking about it when they thought she was in the other room. Some of them blamed her for being too picky and turning him away because he still had a few scars on his body. When one of them called her vain she almost stepped into the room until Sandra spoke up, "Are you guys really so jealous of her that you'd call her vain. If anything the problem's her mate. I need a jacket every time he walks into the room, he's definitely the cold one."

When all the women in the room agreed, Hope bit her lip. Warrick wasn't cold. What he had been through had been traumatic. He was the pack alpha for some of the women in that room and he deserved their respect. If it weren't for him and her brother they would still be living in a rundown with no hope of a future.

Not sure what to say, she had stepped into the room, her head held high. They all froze, a look of horror on their faces wondering what she might have heard. Hope knew she should put them in their place. They would have deserved it but instead she pretended like she hadn't heard them, deciding instead to try and kill them with kindness. When she spoke to Kassandra about it later, Kassandra had told her that if it kept happening she should put her foot down. She pointed out that idle gossip isn't a bad thing but as the alpha's, Warrick and Damien deserved the packs respect. Kassandra smiled at her before saying, "Just like in chess, as a queen your job is to protect the king. You're the only one strong enough."

Hope felt better after her shower. She was going to spend the day with Violca and Kassandra. Violca was throwing her dinner party tomorrow night and somehow the two of them had talked her into getting new clothes to wear. It was supposed to be an informal dinner so she didn't see why they had to go buy new clothes. To be honest, Hope's closet was full of clothes she hadn't worn but the two girls had a way about them that made it hard to say no.

Dressed and ready to go Hope gave herself one last look in the mirror before heading downstairs. Damien's voice was the first one she heard and she smiled. Since meeting his mate her brother had settled down and started to become the man she always knew he was. Not that he was a bad man before, but she was glad the term 'man-whore' was no longer associated with him.

As she heard her name, she paused at the bottom of the stairs, "I'm worried that as long as she is with me she will always be in danger," Warrick said in a hushed toned.

"You really don't give her enough credit," she heard Damien say which made her want to hug him. "You can fight it all you want but the Fates have bound you two and all you're doing is hurting the both of you. Even without the mark she's stuck with you. Always has been. Whether the two of you live together or not she's your mate. You're responsible for her happiness and all you're doing is hurting her... and yourself."

After a moment of silence, Hope proceeded down the stairs and into the kitchen. Damien was the first to look at her. Damien gave her a wink and she realized he'd known that she was there and had overheard part of their conversation. As her cheeks heated up she looked over at Warrick who looked guilty.

"Good morning Damien," she said with an overly bright smile, hoping Warrick didn't notice she was blushing. She kissed her brother on the cheek. "I kind of miss the days you ran the bar and didn't wake up until closer to noon."

Damien chuckled as she made her cup of coffee. "The bar's almost done being built, but Robert's going to run it for me. I'm just going to be a silent partner."

Hope grinned, glancing at Warrick who was quiet. After a few minutes of chatting with her brother the two left. Kassandra and Violca would be coming over in about an hour to pick her up and take her shopping. Her mind went over the conversation she'd overheard. She hadn't heard much, but enough to know that Warrick still worried about his brother, Gabriel. Hope was touched that he worried about her, but she felt like her entire life Gabriel had kept her from the life she wanted and she was no longer willing to live this way. With a slow smile, she decided to stop worrying and instead plot what she would buy on her shopping spree, especially since she'd decided to take Kassandra's advice and seduce Warrick.

9

Warrick thought about Damien's words throughout the day as they finished painting the houses. *Was he just hurting the both of them*? It wasn't like she could just go and be with someone else. Even when she thought he had betrayed her, her wolf had never let anyone touch her. She was a grown woman. If she were human she would probably have grown children of her own and possibly be expecting grandchildren.

In her sleep Hope had responded to his touch. Warrick felt his lips tug up into a grin when he thought about how she had clung to him. Awake with the lights on, Warrick was aware of his every scar, but in his sleep the man and the beast within didn't care about how she deserved someone whole, it just knew she was theirs.

When he woke all the reasons why he shouldn't take her came flooding back. His brother's threats of hurting her were the primary ones. There were times when he woke up that he swore he had heard Gabriel through their twin link. They would need to be close for that to work and, with the constant patrols, Gabriel would have to be a fool to even attempt to come near them.

Laughter from the other side of the house pulled Warrick from his thoughts. Curious who was laughing Warrick got off the ladder to see what was causing it. As he stepped around the corner he saw two kids running around chasing each other with paint on their hands. The two looked like brother and sister, both with the same light blonde hair and brown eyes. The boy looked to be about five years old and the girl couldn't be much older than three. Her little legs were moving as quickly as they could as she chased her brother, white paint on her outstretched hands.

"Ha, ha Mary you can't catch me," the boy said looking over his shoulder taunting his sister as he ran straight toward Warrick.

When the little boy was close Warrick grinned noticing the boy was too busy looking behind him to notice Warrick in front of him. The little guy ran right into his leg causing the boy to fall. Warrick laughed and Mary saw her chance to catch up to her brother, touching him with her white hands.

"I win," she squealed in delight.

Her brother pushed her off him giving her a dirty look as he looked up to see what he'd run into. A look of fear crossed the poor boys face as he began to stammer, "I'm sorry...I didn't."

Warrick gave him his best reassuring smile, not sure what to say to the kid. He'd lowered himself down to help the boy up when he noticed the boy's sister, Mary, looking up at him with big eyes, her lower lip quivering. "Please don't hurt us," Mary said, her big brown eyes filling with tears.

The fact that the two kids were so scared of him worried Warrick. Did he really look that scary? "I wouldn't hurt you," Warrick said as he put his finger in the wet paint on the boy's shirt and tapped Mary's nose.

It was amazing how quickly she went from about to cry, to a look of surprise, before full-blown giggles. "I win," she told him as she pointed at her brother.

The boy frowned. "You only won because I ran into him and fell down."

Warrick reached a hand out to help the boy stand. He couldn't help but notice the slight pause the boy took before finally taking his hand. When he stood, Warrick smiled, "You were too busy looking behind to see what was in front of you. She won fair and square."

Mary beamed up at him before sticking her tongue out at her brother and running away. Before her brother could run after her Warrick stopped him. "It's okay to let your sister win every once in a while. Your job is to protect her." The boy nodded and Warrick pointed to the paint. "Now I believe it is your turn to get her. Just be careful and try to stay in the backyard so you two don't run into anyone else."

With a grin, the boy put his hand in the paint and took off after his sister. The high-pitched squeal was easy to hear. Warrick shook his head and came around the house to see Damien standing there, a grin on his face. "What?" Warrick asked.

"Nothing just wondering how long it's going to take you to look and see what is in front of you." When Warrick frowned, Damien just laughed and walked away, going back to work. With a mock growl Warrick went back to the house deciding to lose himself in his work.

WARRICK GOT home before Hope and took a shower. His thoughts kept going over Damien's words. As the hot water cascaded down his back, he had an image of Hope this morning when she'd asked him to please kiss her.

The thought of being the reason she was in pain cut him like a knife. Warrick could honestly say he would withstand the fires of hell if it meant keeping her safe. He smiled at the memory of her as a child claiming him for herself. It had been a happy memory for so long he'd begun to think he had imagined it.

Dressed in his nicest pair of jeans and a button down black shirt, Warrick finished adjusting his hair in the mirror. He kept going over his conversation with Damien in his head. He would need some time to think about it.

As he stepped out of the room he ran into Hope. She was stepping from her room and his breath caught. She was wearing a pair of black boots that went up to her knees bringing his eyes to the black pants that looked like they could have been painted on. As his eyes followed them up he noticed her top was red, covered with black lace that had metal hooks going up the middle. It reminded him of a sexy version of the corsets women used to wear. It pushed on her breasts, holding them up along with her barely covered nipples. He was torn between staring at her breasts and wanting to cover them up for fear they might pop out. He must have been staring at them for longer than he thought because when he heard her clear her throat, he snapped his eyes up to meet hers. One of her lovely eyebrows was raised and a very teasing smile played on her red lips.

"I'm sorry I didn't know you were home," Warrick said feeling his cheeks heat up at the thought of her catching him staring at her breasts.

"You were in the shower. I hope you don't mind but I brought home dinner. Thought we could eat in the little breakfast nook," Hope said.

"That sounds great," he said giving her a smile. "I'm starving."

Hope smiled and turned to walk down the stairs, leaving him to follow. As she walked, his eyes caressed her from behind. The pants she wore clung to her, cupping her ass in a way that made his mouth water and his hands itch to touch her.

Once downstairs he noticed that she had moved the small table next to the little nook so they could sit on the bench chair in the window. Two candles were lit and he noticed that there were two glasses of red wine along with plates.

"Viktor recommended this steak place. I hope you don't mind," Hope said looking at him over her shoulder.

"It smells delicious," Warrick said as he followed her.

The two of them took a seat on the padded bench and he smiled. The setting was cozy and he was touched by her effort. For the first few minutes they were quiet as they ate. He watched her out of the corner of his eye. There was just enough light coming in from the window that it caused her honey blonde hair to shimmer. He could smell her nervousness despite her best effort to hide it.

"So did you guys find something to wear for Violca's dinner?" Warrick asked, hoping to break the tension.

When Hope didn't answer right away he turned to look at her. Hope wasn't looking at him and he couldn't help but notice the slight flush on her cheeks. "We did," she finally replied and he wondered what the three of them had done that made her blush so.

After a few minutes of silence Hope asked him about his day. When he told her about the two kids he caught playing in the paint she smiled. They talked about the families that had recently moved into their homes. All the families should be in their homes before the end of the year. Hope told him that Kassandra had mentioned a Christmas party to celebrate with both the dragons and the wolves. Warrick's parents would have loved to see the groups getting along so well. All it took was one mating between one of their alphas and one of the personal guards for for things to change. Who would have guessed?

When dinner was finished, he helped her clear the table. As he started to do the dishes he felt her hand on his stopping him.

"I would like to show you what I bought," Hope said, her eyes averted.

Warrick nodded, his mouth going dry as she took his hand in hers and led him up the stairs. Her heeled boots clicked on each floorboard and his eyes trailed down her body. If she bought more clothes like these pants he would need to find something else for her to wear. No way was he going to let others enjoy this view.

When they got to Hope's room she paused and gave him a look. There was a moment of indecision before she pulled him through the door. He hadn't been in her room before. In the center was a big cherry oak four-poster bed. Hope grabbed the single pink bag that was in the center of the bed before walking into her bathroom and closing the door.

Warrick began to look around. The bed was big, bigger than the one in his room, which she had ended up in more often than not. His nightmares kept them both from having a good night's sleep. Despite the first night, when he'd scared her, Hope was brave enough to come into his room every time she heard him having a nightmare. She took the risk, and nothing like that had ever happened again. Instead every morning he woke up kissing her, caressing her skin as he dreamt of a life where nothing stood between them.

Warrick could hear the doorknob turn. As she stepped out, his breath caught. Hope was wearing a small red satin and lace nightdress. The lace was strategically placed, running from under one perfect breast, across her midriff, ending at a partially exposed thigh. His eyes roamed her body. Her long curvy legs were almost completely exposed, the outfit barely long enough to cover the parts of her he longed to see.

As he looked up her body he noticed how her blonde hair brushed the top of the curve of her breasts. His eyes continued up noticing that the red of her lipstick matched the tight nightgown that he so badly wanted to rip from her body. He saw her teeth gently bite her lower lip before he looked up into her eyes. Her pupils were so dilated they almost looked black. She didn't meet his gaze, instead he noticed her eyes shift around the room. For the first time he could see how she stood perfectly still, holding her breath as if she was waiting for him to say something.

"You're beautiful," he whispered as he took a step toward her.

Warrick watched as Hope let out a breath before meeting his eyes. He wasn't sure what to expect next when she finally spoke, her voice so quiet it was barely a whisper. "I think you should sleep here tonight, in *our* bed."

The words our bed echoed in his head. Taking the last step toward her, he cupped her cheek forcing her to look at him. Every reason why he should stay away from her meant nothing if he was hurting her. She stood before him like a goddess, all he could see was the vulnerable look in her eyes, and he knew that he was the one who had put it there. "Are you sure?"

Hope's lip curved in a small smile as she leaned into him. He felt her hand slide up his chest and wrap around the back of his neck. As she pulled him down she whispered the one word that was his complete undoing, "Please."

10

Hope felt his body stiffen a moment before his mouth finally came down and joined hers. Warrick's thumb stroked her cheek as his hand held in her place. He tilted her head up for better access as his tongue slid into her mouth. This kiss was different from the others, and not just because it started when he was awake. No, this one had the promise of everything she had been dreaming about for the past few years.

When he broke the kiss, she whimpered, trying to pull his head back down to her. When she finally opened her eyes she saw he was breathing as hard as she was. Warrick released her and she felt him turn his body as he reached behind her and turned off the light in the bathroom.

His body shifted and she let out a surprised yelp as he grabbed her under the knees and lifted her off the ground with ease. His chest rumbled under hers as he carried her to the bed.

"Are you scared, Hope?" he asked, his breath on her ear causing her to shudder.

"No," she whispered as she turned to look at him. "I know you'd never do anything to hurt me."

Warrick paused and for a moment she thought she might have

gone too far when he suddenly brushed his lips against hers. He lowered her slowly to the bed placing her close to the middle. She felt the bed dip as he stretched out next to her. She felt his hand slowly slide up and down her arm until they laced with her fingers. "As beautiful as this is on you, I do hope this isn't what you decided to wear to tomorrow's dinner."

A giggle escaped her as she teased, "I bought a black one just like this, thinking it would look more formal for dinner."

She heard his mock growl as he leaned down, his breath feathering her lip. "If that's the case I'm afraid we'll be cancelling our plans to go out tomorrow."

With that, he kissed her. Soft and sweet, her body arched up to his as he leaned partially over her. She slid her leg up his and while feeling the material of his jeans against her she realized how naked she was compared to him.

Hope released his hand, while still kissing him and slid hers up his arm and into his hair. So involved in the kiss she didn't realize where his hand was until she felt it slide up her thigh to her hip. When he broke the kiss she whimpered and he smiled as he nibbled on her lips. "There were times when I'd dream about you. Imagine how soft your skin would be under my fingers." Hope gasped as his fingers slowly traced patterns on her hip. "Your skin feels better than I'd ever imagined."

His words made her blush as her hips arched under his touch. Hope felt his mouth curl in a smile against her skin as her body reacted to his. Warrick's lips slid to her ear where he nibbled, causing her to shudder. "I feel like you're over dressed," she whispered glad the lights were off.

Warrick pulled back looking at her and she felt the bed shift as he got up. The room was too dark to see much and she watched him pull his shirt off and toss it to the chair on the side of the room. As he undid his pants her breath caught. The zipper was so loud in the quiet room. When he pushed down his jeans she found herself disappointed that his boxers had stayed on.

Warrick stood next to the bed, the light from outside shining down on him, and she worried that he had changed his mind and was about to walk out and leave her here alone and needy. When he finally joined her back in the bed she had to bite her cheek to stop herself from saying *thank you* out loud.

Hope smiled at him as she reached up and brought his face back to hers. "I used to dream about you too."

When he paused she brushed her lips against his. "I would wake up, my body aching for you and I was so mad you weren't with me."

"I'm here now," Warrick whispered. She smiled against his lips in response as she pulled him closer, kissing him deep.

The two kissed until she was breathless, his hands lightly roaming her body. Skimming over the parts of her body that wanted more contact. Hope, feeling restless, released his head and slid her hands down his chest. When she reached a nipple she flicked it with her nail. His sharp inhale made her giggle and break the kiss. Her other hand did it to the other nipple to see if he would react the same. Hope almost giggled again but instead a moan escaped her as he reached up to squeeze her breast in return.

"I wonder if you...," he started to ask as he flicked her nipple just like she did his. Her back arched up off the bed as she gasped in pleasure.

"Beautiful," he whispered as his lips traveled down her neck to her chest. She felt him cover her breast with his mouth for the first time over the thin silky material. With her hands pressed between their two bodies, they curved slightly as she felt him suck.

The material felt wet when he pulled back. She moaned, pulling his hair only to sigh when his mouth firmly closed on the second one, treating it to the same delicious torment he had the first. Each wonderful flick and suck caused her stomach muscles to quiver and that spot between her legs to feel empty.

"Warrick," she whispered. Hope could hear the need in her own voice.

She wished she had some experience in this area. She ran her hand down his chest, her fingers playing across his lower stomach. When she tentatively traced it with her fingers she felt him stiffen.

His hand left her breast and covered her hands before pulling them up and over her head. He shifted and settled between her thighs, still holding her hands over her head. "I want to touch you," she whispered.

His breath was coming in short little pants as he put his forehead against hers. "Stay still," he growled as he looked down at her. Warrick didn't move, just watched her. When she nodded, he released her hands and slid his lips along her jaw. He kissed his way down her neck causing her to arch her back up against him. His hands brushed her breast and this time her hips came up off the bed bumping against his cock, causing him to hiss.

His hand slid up her thigh pushing the nightgown up with it. When he got to the top he pulled it up and over and her head. He paused, looking her over. Even in the dark she knew he could see her. Warrick was a wolf and if he wanted to see her with the little light coming in through the windows she knew his wolf would have no problem. "Stunning," he whispered.

Hope blushed then turned her head and she felt him nuzzle the side of her neck. His hands low on her belly just above the thin material of the pretty red lace underwear that came with the nightgown. They were modest with hints of lace leading to where the satin material just barely covered her. "You still have a chance to say no Hope, before we go too far."

Hope looked up at him and cupped his cheek. She felt him tense when she touched his scar. "I need you Warrick. Please don't stop."

There was a long pause and for the first time that night she called upon her wolf to help her see him better. His thoughts were on display for her to see. Warrick was battling his own demons. He almost looked defeated and she thought about taking her words back when he finally nodded.

Warrick bent down and kissed her gently this time. This kiss was soft, light, as his hands skimmed her body. When she felt his hand on her hips she rolled them encouraging him to touch her. There was an ache, an emptiness inside her.

His lips trailed down the side of her jaw going lower. For the first time his fingers skimmed on the satin covering her between her thighs. A whimper escaped her and she felt her hips move on their own trying to deepen the contact. She had spent many nights touching herself, dreaming of this moment. When his fingers finally slid under the material she felt them slide along her wet fold.

Not sure how to ask him for what she wanted, she spread her thighs wider as her hips bucked under his fingers. His ragged breathing the only thing letting her know he was as affected as she was. His long thick finger slid inside her and she cried out, her hands gripping the sheets.

"Did I hurt you?" Warrick asked. His voice sounded strained as she felt his finger unmoving, buried inside of her.

"No," she whispered realizing he was as new to this as she was. She rolled her hips up encouraging him.

Warrick looked down at her and she could see him studying her face as he slowly moved his finger, pulling out before slowly pushing back. A moan of pleasure escaped her but she wanted more. When he slid in a second finger her hands went to his shoulders and she gripped him tight.

Hope was aware of him watching her, as if he was studying her reaction to every touch. He continued his delicious slow torment on her body until her hips were moving on their own. He dipped his head and began to kiss along her jaw, up to her ear, biting gently. Turning her head, she captured his lips with a kiss. Pouring her desire into the kiss she sucked on his tongue. He growled in response and she moaned.

Unable to hold back anymore, she broke the kiss. "Warrick… I need you please."

He moved his finger and she felt the bed shift as he removed his boxers. Settling between her thighs she felt his cock slide between her wet folds and her hips cradled him. Every time he shifted his hip she moaned before he finally reached down and positioned the head of his cock at her entrance.

Hope looked him in the eye. The light gleam let her know he was looking at her through his wolf eyes and she tilted her head in an act of submission, offering him her neck. "Now...Warrick."

He thrust in hard. Entering her in one quick move and this time she cried out in pain. Her body protesting for a moment from the invasion. Warrick tensed, not moving and she heard him whisper, "I'm sorry, I didn't mean to hurt you."

Her body shifted as he held perfectly still above her. Hope moved again and this time she felt pleasure from his slight movement in her body. "It's better now," she whispered.

When he didn't move, Hope looked up at him to see the strain on his face as he held still. Shifting her hips again she heard his slight moan as a curious feeling of pleasure hit her. She repeated the move, this time a moan of her own escaped as she slid her hands up his arms to his shoulders.

"Hope, oh gods," Warrick gritted between his teeth as he started to move. Her head rested on his shoulder as she ran her hands down his back and her hips moved up on their own to meet every wonderful thrust.

"Warrick, my Warrick," she whispered.

She could feel that he was holding back and that thought annoyed her. When her hands slid to his ass she gripped him tighter, begging him to move a little faster. His grunt was the only sound he made before she felt him pick up speed.

She kissed and bit along his shoulder. When he hit a particular spot inside her, she gasped. Warrick slowed his movement and Hope was so close to experiencing what she had always heard about, got mad, turning her head and biting his neck. Hard. Breaking the skin.

With a growl his hips started pounding into her harder, more forceful and wickedly delightful. When the metallic taste of his blood hit her tongue, she moaned and felt him shift as he bit the base of her neck, his teeth sinking into her. The pleasure pain was too much for her and she screamed as she felt her entire body tighten and go over.

Lost in her own bliss she barely heard his muffled growl. The sudden flood of heat in her core and the frantic movement of his hips meeting hers let her know he was experiencing the same pleasure.

Slowly Hope became aware of her body starting to come down. The small tremors of her stomach muscles and the little quivering she felt around him when he twitched deep inside her would have embarrassed her if she wasn't feeling so good.

As she released his neck she gave in to the urge and licked him. When his cock kicked hard inside her she grinned and slowly ran her tongue up his neck. Warrick slowly released her neck and did the same to her. She realized that his mark was going to be in the middle of the neck, she'd bitten him hard and they would all know she was lost in her pleasure when he received it. For some odd reason that thought made her smile as she licked him one more time, a low moan escaping her as she felt him repeating her action.

11

Warrick moaned as he copied her actions and licked the base of her neck where he'd bitten. Hope's moan made his cock kick hard inside and when he moved he felt her wince softly. Feeling bad for hurting her he pulled out and was surprised when he felt her lips frown against his neck. "Your body needs to rest."

As he pulled back to look down at her he instantly missed the feel of her lips against his skin. A small smile playing on her lips made him feel a swell of pride. He was the reason she currently had that dazed look on her face. "I'll be right back," he said getting up to go the bathroom. Finding a washcloth, he got it wet to clean himself up. The tiny bit of blood on his cock reminded him that he had hurt her. Quickly cleaning himself, he grabbed a clean cloth and wet it. Bringing it to the bed he quickly cleaned her up as well.

There was a small wince as he started to clean her up and he felt like she might pull away so he put his hand on her hip. "Let me," he simply stated and she nodded. Once she was clean he put away the used cloth before climbing back into bed with her.

Hope looked like a beautiful angel waiting for him. Her blonde hair fanned out on the pillow and when he crawled back in bed with her, she rolled over to put her head on his chest. Warrick slid his fingers through her hair as she lay in his arms. There was a part of him that thought he should feel guilty for taking her innocence but the way she screamed and responded to his touch had made him feel...alive.

"Warrick," he heard her whisper his name, making him pause.

"Yes, Hope?" he asked feeling a little uncertain.

"I think you should move from that room to this room –– our room."

He kissed the top of her head thinking about her request. "Are you sure that's what you want?"

Before looking up at him, Hope kissed the top of his chest, right above where his heart beat steadily. "You're my mate Warrick. I know things didn't start like they should but I think we should move forward...together."

Warrick picked up on her nervousness. She was asking him for what he had been imagining for as long as he could remember. But his brother was still out there. He still felt the connection to him. Gabriel would be able to feel that he had finally claimed Hope as his mate. Warrick claiming Hope put her in harm's way even more than before and marking her might have been both the most wonderful and selfish thing he had ever done in his entire life.

"Hope I..." he started to say and then felt her hand go up and rest on his cheek. Stopping him from continuing, she shook her head.

"Your brother's our problem. Not yours alone. I'm your mate, a member of your pack, and he's been hurting our people. He's not your burden alone."

As Hope spoke, he felt her fingers find his scar and he tried to pull back but Hope wouldn't let him. She picked her head up and he bit back a growl. She ran her tongue along his scar before looking up at him and then brushed her lips against his.

"If anything happened to you," Warrick started to say as she brushed her lips back and forth across his. Every pass of those lips, melted his resolve a little more. "Promise me you'll leave if there's a sign of my brother."

Hope smiled against his lips and she shook her head. "I'm your mate, your better half," she said as she nibbled on his lips. "You should know I'd never run. Please don't leave me Warrick. I've waited for you my entire life, dreamt of you and missed something I never had. Fight for me – *with* me."

Warrick didn't know what to say. He pulled back just enough to look down at her. The moonlight coming in from the window seemed to glow in her eyes. The hint of her wolf underneath knew that both the animal and the woman needed him to say something. With a sigh he nodded. "Whatever happens, for now we handle it together, as mates."

The tension he felt coming from her melted away. Even in the dark he could see her smile was dazzling, then she came up and kissed him deeply. He moaned as her soft body pressed into his and he wanted nothing more than to take her again. To kiss every inch of her delicious body. He had dreamt of taking her a hundred times. Each dream more creative than the next, doing things he had never imagined in his youth.

His hand skimmed over her body and he remembered a comment his father had made about how a woman's body needed a bit of time to heal after their first time. Warrick broke the kiss and smiled when he heard Hope growl in response. "Sleep, it's been a long day."

As he spoke, he tucked her body against his. Despite his good intention his cock was rock hard and when she turned in his arms Hope pulled his arm around her, holding him close. When she wiggled, he moaned as his cock nestled between the perfect globes that were her ass. When she moved again he knew the little minx was doing it on purpose and he pulled his hand free to smack her ass. "Behave," he growled.

Her soft giggle made him smile and he nipped at the back of her neck. When she shuddered he did it again. "You are going to be a handful aren't you my darling Hope?"

He felt her head tilt and he pictured her thinking about it. "If you're lucky I'll be two handfuls."

Warrick laughed. His hand slid up to her breast and he cupped one, feeling the weight. He heard her soft intake of breath. "I guess I'm very lucky indeed. But for now, I'd like my mate to get some sleep. I know she's been working very hard for her people and tomorrow she's going to introduce me to the vampire who I'm going to have to thank for keeping her safe."

Hope relaxed in his arms and he listened to her breathing. After a bit he finally felt her body relax and her breathing even out. Warrick almost laughed. He wanted nothing more than to take her again but she needed to sleep and he knew he should too. He doubted she had gotten more than three hours a night since they'd moved in together. Most nights he woke her up with his nightmares…or his body reacting to hers after she crawled in bed with him. Surrounded by her scent Warrick finally fell asleep.

He knew this dream was different the moment it started.

The sun was shining and he was standing on the front porch watching himself in the yard. He was smiling as he chased a little girl around the yard. Her happy squeal of delight echoed as he swept her off her feet and tossed her into the air, catching her. As the little girl laughed, two little boys came running out of the house yelling.

The boys ran right through him like he wasn't even there. He heard laughter coming from the house and turned to see a very pregnant Hope walking outside. Her hand on her belly as she stepped out from the screen door. He reached out to touch her and passed through her like a ghost. He watched her for a moment as she watched the other him in the yard with the three kids. There was a look of love in her eyes as she sat on the porch swing.

After a few minutes Warrick watched the kids run off together and his other self walked up to her on the porch. Placing a hand on her belly he leaned down and gave her a kiss that was both sweet and very arousing.

"This one seems to be ready to come out and play with his sister and cousins," the other him said while he nibbled on Hope's lips.

Hope smiled up at him nodding. "I believe you're right. This one gets all excited every time the kids are making noise."

Warrick watched as he sat next to her and the way the two held each other tight. There was something intimate in this moment that he felt like he was spying on himself and intruding on their privacy.

As he turned to leave he heard the door open again and this time an older woman came out of the house and was staring straight at him. "Warrick, where are you going?"

Warrick felt a sense of surprise when he realized it was Hope's mother. Her blonde hair had hints of grey and she had a few lines around her eyes he didn't remember her having when he'd met her years ago. Not sure what to say or how, out of everyone here only she could see him, so he just shrugged. She smiled at him shaking her head. "You have two choices Warrick. You can fight for this life and be happy or you can run away and let your brother win and make both you and my daughter miserable."

"What if she gets hurt?" he whispered, not sure why he was even answering her.

She gave him a look of sympathy before looking over at the couple sitting on the porch swing, "You've fought to stay alive and protect her from your brother. Being apart from you and thinking you betrayed her was worse than anything your brother could do to her. I'm sorry you had to endure that...and I'm sorry for what is to come. But for the sake of my daughter I hope you're strong enough to realize that together the two of you are stronger."

Before he could ask her what she meant she disappeared. He wanted to know what was to come, how to protect her. When he looked back at the couple on the porch he felt his heart ache with the promise of a future with her. Hope looked lovingly up at his dream self and whispered, "I love you Warrick."

∾

WARRICK WOKE up to the sound of Hope's steady breathing as she lay across his chest. Her leg was tucked between his and her breast felt perfect pressed against his chest. The memory of her big and pregnant in his dreams made him smile. He wondered if she might already be pregnant. Shaking his head, he thought to himself that he would like to enjoy some time of just the two of them before they started adding children. He felt greedy and a bit selfish but for now, if they were going to do this, he wanted her to himself. Warrick just needed to get rid of his brother to do that.

Untangling himself from her arms Warrick kissed hope on the forehead pushing back her hair. She looked innocent in her sleep and the light coming in from the window made it look like she had a halo. Warrick smiled thinking that under the halo she was a siren that called to him. Warrick gave her one last look and for a moment debated about waking her up with kisses.

Hope had often been woken up in the middle of the night by his nightmares and he decided to let her enjoy sleeping in. He had some errands to run this morning but they both agreed to be home early to get ready for tonight's dinner. She was excited to have him meet Lazzaro, the vampire king, who raised had her and Damien.

Warrick went into his room, grabbed a pair of jeans and a plain t-shirt, putting them on before he went downstairs. A nice breakfast in bed would be a perfect way to show Hope he meant to give it a try with her. His dream gave him a flicker of what life could be together. He could still hear her whispering she loved him and he wanted to hear those words on her lips more than anything.

Rummaging in the kitchen Warrick found pancake mix and bacon. He also knew that Hope loved her coffee in the morning and preferred those sweet flavored creamers she kept readily on hand. His dad had often made their mother breakfast in bed and had taught him on Mother's Day. "Bacon," he said was always first. He smiled remembering his dad. "You can always remember to cook bacon first because it's the most important part of breakfast, Son."

Warrick, in the beginning, had often thought of his parents after their deaths. He wondered why they never saw it coming with his brother. He often wondered why he didn't see his brother's jealousy.

He never even knew that his brother had met a witch. There was a twin link between the two and he knew his brother was often mad about something but when he asked him about it he would always say it was because of something else. Not able to see it, or maybe he just didn't want to, Warrick often just shrugged it off. Now he wondered if he could have done something different or was that hate for him, being born second, always just going to be a part of Gabriel?

The bacon done, Warrick started the coffee and made the pancakes. Having preheated the oven to its lowest temperature he put them inside to keep warm as he piled them in a big stack. Warrick decided four big pancakes each with bacon were enough for them both.

A sound from the stairs drew his attention and he turned to see Hope standing there wearing his shirt from last night. There was something sexy about the look. Her hair was tousled from last night's activity, and he took her all in. He noticed her amber eyes were shining after a good night's rest and her cheeks were a rosy pink. He almost moaned out loud when he saw she wasn't wearing a bra and her hard nipples were poking through the material. Hope had long legs and his shirt covered her just enough. He wondered if there was anything else she forgot to put on.

"I was going to bring you breakfast in bed," Warrick said when Hope glanced at the plates on the counter.

The little smile that was playing on her lips grew until she was beaming at him. "I love pancakes," she said taking a step toward him.

When she stood before him she put her arms around his neck pulling him down for a kiss. Warrick moaned as he brought his lips to hers. He could kiss her from now to the day he died and he would never get tired of her taste, the way her body molded to his. She was heaven.

"I was worried when I woke up and you weren't there, but then the smell of bacon called to me and I had to see what you were doing," she said after breaking the kiss. Warrick felt her hand slide from his back to his neck where her fingers found her mark on him. There was a wave of awareness as she teasingly traced her bite mark.

Warrick felt bad for worrying her and looked at the base of her neck. He could see the frenzy in his bite mark on her skin. Bending his head, Warrick trailed his lips along the side of her neck until he came to his mark on her skin and nipped playfully. Her sharp inhale followed by the tightening of her fingers in his hair made him smile. When he heard her stomach grumble letting him know that his mate was hungry, he chuckled. "Come let's eat our breakfast before it gets cold. I was about to make you a cup of coffee with some of your fancy creamer."

Hope pulled back and the smile she gave him made him feel like the biggest hero. Warrick poured them both a cup of coffee. Keeping his black, he watched as she got salted caramel creamer from the fridge and proceeded to turn her black coffee into something that looked closer to chocolate milk. He shook his head and let her carry the coffee cups as he took the plates and they went into the living room.

Hope sat next to him on the couch and he watched as she ate her breakfast. A drop of syrup on her lips brought them to his attention and when her tongue came out and licked it he fought the urge to lean over and kiss her. He wanted to smile as he realized that he let go of his control for her. Now *wanted* to do all those things that came to him in his dreams. Not sure how she would feel, he shook his head.

"Anything I should know about Lazzaro tonight before I meet him?" he asked, curious about the vampire who raised her.

He could see Hope's grin as she thought about it. "He likes to push buttons. For some reason flirting with Violca and Aithne, knowing he is pissing off the dragons, amuses him. He really doesn't mean anything by it. Lazzaro thinks the mating between two people is sacred and would never do anything to compromise that. He just enjoys watching their reactions."

Warrick shook his head. "So he enjoys poking the... dragon, so to speak."

Hope laughed, nodding. "He says people are the most sincere when you get them riled up. You can tell what's important to a man by what he's willing to defend. Plus, he admires Violca. When he met her for the first time he told me how she wasn't rattled by him. A witch who doesn't know how to use her powers was willing to go out on her own and meet with him to protect her family."

"Lazzaro is used to people being scared of him?" Warrick asked. He knew the reputation of the previous vampire king even as a teenager. His parents had said that he was known for having bouts of rage and killing hundreds in his wake.

"Lazzaro is surrounded by people who would like nothing more than to see him fail. They want to go back to the old ways of feeding off humans. There have been bombings on some of the blood banks and attacks on Lazzaro's most loyal supporters. They aren't as afraid of him as his father since he is not as ruthless, but I think they decided to play it safe and not attack him directly, instead looking for his weakness and trying to exploit them."

Warrick was surprised by the depth of Hope's knowledge. "You know a lot about what was going on. How did he keep you safe when you guys were kids?" Warrick asked, curious.

"He hid us away with a very well paid nanny and staff that he trusted. He visited when he could. More so when we were really young and I was scared."

"I only knew his father by reputation. But I'm glad he's nothing like him and that he raised you. When everything first went down I believed you were killed. When I found out you were alive I wondered how it was you both managed to escape. You were so young."

Hope gave him a tentative smile then leaned over, brushing his lips with hers while whispering, "You were young too. But we have plenty of time to make up for the life we've missed out on so far. Let's get our revenge on your brother by showing him how happy we can be."

Warrick smiled against her lips when he felt her move their plates. She kept her lips softly brushing back and forth against his. She straddled his lap and kissed him deeply. Her movement was bolder than she was last night. Her hands slid into his hair and he felt her hold him as her tongue slid into his mouth. Trying to coax his tongue into hers.

With a moan Warrick gave himself over to the kiss. Sliding his hand up her thighs marveling at how smooth her skin felt, his tongue dueled with hers, tasting the syrup she had just eaten making her taste just that much sweeter.

As his hands made their way up her thighs he grabbed her ass and felt that she was wearing nothing under his shirt. As his hands grabbed her two perfect globes he growled his approval, pulling her close to him. His cock pressing hard against the fly of his jeans.

Her soft gasp against his mouth turned into a moan as she began to move her hips in a delicious way so she was grinding on his cock. When she took over that movement his hands were free to roam as they pleased and they slid from her waist up to her breasts. He broke the kiss to replace his hands with his mouth and taste the nipples that had been teasing him all morning.

Warrick loved the sounds she made as she arched her back. As he pushed her shirt up he heard the door open and Damien's voice. "I told you we had time to make love one more time this morning."

Hope made a high-pitched noise he could only call a squeal as she jumped off his lap and ran down the hall to the stairs. Damien walked into the living room chuckling shaking his head as Kassandra smacked him on his arm. "You didn't have to embarrass her."

Warrick watched as Damien pulled Kassandra into his arms smiling. "After all the times she interrupted me…"

Kassandra raised an eyebrow stopping him with a look. "Should I ask you about these women that left such a vivid memory that you felt like you owed your sister payback?"

Damien gave Kassandra a boyish grin, pulling her close and whispering, "Just practice for you my love."

Kassandra rolled her eyes, pushing him away while giving him an apologetic grin. "I'm sorry Warrick. I should have realized why he was so eager for me to get out of bed this morning and visit with you."

Warrick wasn't sure what to say. Mostly he was glad that his cock seemed to have deflated when they walked into the room. "If you two don't mind I am going to go upstairs and check on Hope."

As he walked upstairs he heard Damien call out after him, "Put a shirt on"

Warrick chuckled as he ran up the stairs two at a time. Grabbing a shirt first from his room he walked across the hall, knocking on Hopes door. Not hearing anything he slowly opened the door to find her sitting on the bed. She took one look at him and started laughing.

For a split second, he wondered if something was really wrong but she jumped up and threw herself in his arms. Warrick took a step back as he got his footing. Holding her tight, she laughed in his arms. The sound brought a smile to his lips.

"Are you okay?" he asked after a few minutes of just holding her.

Hope pulled back, looking down at him, a smile on her lips as her amber eyes seemed to almost dance with mischievousness. This was the girl he remembered. Eyes shining bright and a smile that seemed to tease her lips. Her happiness was so bright it was contagious and he smiled back at her. One hand slid and cupped his cheek and he winced slightly when he felt her fingers trace the scar on his face. "I'm perfect," she whispered before brushing her lips against his.

When he put her down he missed her in his arms. This was all new to him and he didn't want to mess it up. "Should I tell your brother to leave?"

He watched the light shine off her as she shook her head, "No, he's just getting me back for every time I embarrassed him."

Hope gave him another kiss and he could feel her smiling under his lips. "Go downstairs. I'll be there in a minute."

Warrick gave her one more look before nodding and heading downstairs. When he got into the living room he saw a note on the table. Picking it up he almost laughed when he saw what was written on it, *It's about time. Kassandra says Congratulations. We will see you tonight at dinner.*

He laughed as he read it over. Damien had treated him more like a brother than his own brother had, and he enjoyed the teasing the two of them shared. The reminder about dinner made him nervous.

Tonight, he would be meeting the man Hope thought of like a father. He was happy to thank him for saving her, but that weird queasy feeling in his stomach wouldn't go away. He just hoped tonight went off without a hitch. As he walked back toward the stairs he realized that he and his mate were alone and it made him smile as he went up the stairs.

12

The dinner was to be informal but Hope still wanted to look nice. She chose a pair of black jeans that hugged her just perfectly and a black and gold blouse. She left her hair down, curling it slightly on the bottom, and applied just a hint of makeup. Keeping it simple she went with red lipstick and mascara then she checked herself out one more time.

She felt a pair of eyes watching her and she looked up and smiled at Warrick leaning in the doorway. His eyes roamed over her body and she felt herself blush under his gaze. After her brother left, he came upstairs to join her and she thought he was going to take her again. She was a bit disappointed when he only kissed her and told her that he had some things he needed to get done and left her to go out.

Warrick returned a few hours later and she watched him in the mirrors reflection. His shirt was white and the top button was left unbuttoned. He had freshly shaved and his shoulder length hair was combed back. His slacks looked molded to his legs. Over the past few weeks, with his wolf healing ability and working on rebuilding the town, his muscles had developed nicely. She could still see a bit of a limp when he walked but it did not take away from the fact that when he walked you knew he was a predator. The way he was watching her now made her feel like she was his prey and she wanted nothing more than to be caught.

When he was behind her, she noticed his hands come up doing something behind her. The angle of the mirror didn't let her see what he was doing and she fought the urge to turn around and look. When his hands finally came up and over her head she was surprised to see he was putting a necklace on her. Hope brought her hands under her hair picking it up and out of the way for him as he clasped it.

When he was done she looked at the reflection in the mirror. The necklace had two gold wolves that were cuddled together. Hope looked at him over her shoulder and smiled, "It's beautiful. Where'd you get it?"

Watching Warrick, she was aware of the slight pull of his lips. He looked happy at her reaction. "I was helping one of the families move into a home the other day. She was the daughter of one of my mother's best friends. Her mother found some of my mother's jewelry and managed to keep it hidden. She had it stored in a box and asked me to come by because she wanted to give it back to me."

Hope smiled, her fingers tracing over the two wolves. Tilting her head up, she reached out to pull his face to hers and kissed him gently. "I love it. Thank you."

Warrick slid his hands around her waist pulling her back, tighter against his chest. He brushed his lips along the back of her neck and she shivered, loving the feather light touch. "We better get going. Your brother will be waiting for us at his house. If we're late he'll make sure everyone knows why."

A giggle escaped Hope as she nodded her head in agreement. "I think he'll enjoy telling everyone why we are late. He's waited years to embarrass me."

Hope felt happier than she could ever remember feeling as Warrick placed his hand on her back and led her out of the room. They were quiet as they drove over to Damien's and Kassandra's. Since Kassandra and Damien would be moving soon into the house next to theirs the two had been debating about selling the house and using the money to help the pack. After much debate, Kassandra decided instead of selling her house she would lend it out as a halfway house for other shifters that needed temporary housing after an attack from the Orion hunters. More and more families were losing their homes and needed a place to go.

As they pulled up she saw Damien and Kassandra on the porch. Kassandra looked stunning in a pair of snug black, low-rise jeans and a red blouse that had a scoop neck showing off just a hint of her generous cleavage. The outfit was complete with a pair of heeled boots that Hope loved. Her brother, true to form, was wearing all black. As a couple, they looked stunning together.

Hope got out of the car and Damien called out to her as he walked down the porch stairs. "I was about to go to your house and see if you two needed a douse of cold water."

Kassandra rolled her eyes, shaking her head. "Will you leave them alone."

Damien laughed pulling her close, nuzzling her neck as he whispered something that made Kassandra laughed.

Hope smiled as she looked at Warrick out of the corner of her eye. He was smiling before Warrick said back, "You two look a little busy. We can just tell everyone you couldn't make it."

Damien chuckled and took Kassandra's hand leading her toward his truck. "I'm driving," he said with a grin.

Kassandra told Warrick to sit in front as she got in the back. Hope got in and smiled, blushing when Kassandra gave her a very happy smile. "You look beautiful," Kassandra told her after they were all seated and Damien pulled away.

"Thank you," Hope said knowing she still had the same goofy smile she'd had on all day. The two of them chatted in the back as their mates discussed what work was still left to be done. All the homes were finished except for Damien's and Kassandra's, which they had requested to be built last. The downtown section of town had old rundown stores and they had finished most of the wiring and rebuilding of those buildings. The town was starting to come together and everyone seemed to have fallen into their jobs easily.

Going through the gate to Viktor's house, Hope looked around to see if she could see Lazzaro's car. He would be one of the last to show up since he couldn't travel when the sun was at its highest. His special tinted windows worked well but weren't able to block out all the light. This left him to travel either early in the morning or closer to dusk if he chose to drive himself. If he sat in the back and had a driver he was covered better since it was the front window that had to have very specialized glass so as not to be pulled over by the police.

Knocking on the door Hope smiled when Eva answered. With her dark hair and laughing blue eyes Eva greeted them with a big hug. She was the second oldest of the witch sisters and was finishing up her second year of college. "Violca is in the living room with the rest of the gang."

"Lazzaro isn't here yet, is he?" Hope asked, knowing if he'd arrived early he would have parked in the garage.

With a noncommittal shrug, Eva shook her head. "I don't think so. I just got here a few minutes ago and was about to check on the food when I heard you guys at the door."

Kassandra gave her a big grin. "You look beautiful."

Hope had to agree with her. Eva was wearing a blue blouse that made her eyes stand out even more. They were already a lovely shade of blue but with the emerald blouse on you could see them from across the room. Her black hair was only partially up, with a few ringlets framing her face. Hope noticed she was wearing more makeup than usual. Normally she wore just lipstick but today she had eyeliner that further enhanced her eyes and a shade of lipstick that definitely made her pouty lips look more kissable.

"Do you have a date after dinner?" Hope asked, deciding she looked like she was definitely trying to get someone's attention.

"No," she said shaking her head, smoothing her hands over her dark jeans as she led them down the hall to the living room.

The men could be heard through the door and Hope smiled. Tonight there would be Viktor, the dragon king, and his queen Aithne, Chase and Violca, Scott and Eryk, the panther shifter brothers, Eva and Lazzaro, and of course, the four of them. At one table there would be two kings, a dragon, and a vampire, two alpha wolves, panther shifters, and the witches who brought them all together.

Hope would have never thought a union like this was possible. All supernaturals tend to stick to their own kind. With rivalries going back long before most of them were born. It took orphaned witches, who didn't even know about magic, or supernaturals to bring them all together. A group of five females, all descendants of the first witch, possibly destined to change the world. They were already breaking so many rules; including the one that said only one female witch could be born from each set of parents. Normally males would be less powerful than the female. It must be interesting to live in a family where the strongest were women.

Eva opened the door and everyone looked to them. Violca, a warm welcoming smile on her face, was the first to greet them, followed shortly thereafter by Chase. Viktor, always a little more reserved, hung back and waited until the rest of the group said their hellos. Hope watched as Viktor shook Warrick's hand. "You look like you're doing much better."

Warrick nodded. "Again, thank you for all your help. The town is starting to thrive."

Viktor shrugged him off and Aithne smiled at them, "We're very glad to hear it. Don't let him fool you."

Viktor raised an eyebrow giving Aithne a look that simply made her smirk in reply. Aithne's name meant fire. Hope loved watching when the light hit her flaming red hair, she truly looked like she was surrounded by fire, fitting for the dragon queen. Her bright green eyes and her height made Aithne stand out. She was one of the few females that stood almost as tall as Viktor. She was the daughter of Boudicca, saved by a goddess who had made her and her sisters immortal. Aithne was a trained warrior and Hope often smiled thinking that the Fates definitely had an interesting way of picking ones mates. She glanced at Warrick and she couldn't help but think they enjoyed turning one's life upside down.

Hope felt, sadly, like she was lacking something, surrounded by these strong females. Violca was bringing groups together that before would have never thought about talking. Aithne was an assassin, hired by Lazzaro to kidnap Chase before she mated with the king. Even Kassandra was a guard to the king. Hope, however, was basically Lazzaro's secretary. Lately, she wasn't even that because she was helping the town get ready.

Smiling, Eva came up next to Hope and handed her a glass of red wine. Hope knew Eva was a telepath who had learned to block out most thoughts. She had told her that supernaturals were harder to read. For a moment, Hope thought Eva might have read her mind before shaking it off. Eva was very good about trying to respect everyone's privacy.

"I drove through town yesterday. It looks so different. You guys must be so proud," Eva said as she sipped her own drink.

Hope gave her a smile, nodding, "We are. The people all look like they're happy. It's interesting seeing such a big change in the way they carry themselves."

Eva nodded, quickly agreeing. Hope looked around smiling when she saw Warrick talking to Chase. The two of them got along very well and he had told her that Chase used to help him walk around when he first started to heal.

She would never be able to thank Chase and Violca enough. Violca used her healing ability and Hope had often seen her come out of the room looking exhausted. Violca had the natural ability of healing so even though she was still learning how to use her magic, just her touch was enough to heal someone. Her instinct took over and she was able to use the mating connection with Chase, and her natural connection with her sisters to pull more power to help heal him.

Warrick looked up at her and smiled, causing her to blush. When she looked up she noticed Eva grinning. "You two look like you're doing much better."

Hope smiled, opening her mouth to change the subject when a knock was heard at the door. Viktor excused himself to go answer the door. It was impossible not to notice the slight change in the air. Lazzaro loved getting under people's skin. Violca smiled as she laced her arm through Chase's and smiled at Hope. "I really hope you plan on telling us, during dinner, embarrassing stories of Lazzaro from when you were younger."

Hope was laughing when Lazzaro walked in the door and his slight frown made her laugh even harder. "I hope you are not laughing at me, my cucciola."

She beamed at him before walking over and hugging him tight. Lazzaro used to affectionately call her his puppy in Italian when she was younger. He hadn't called her that in years but this was the longest she had gone without seeing him and she had missed him terribly. His silver blonde hair was slicked back. Everyone always thought his demeanor was cold but he had always been warm and affectionate with her. She thought he was a giant when she was younger. He was still tall, well over six feet and the tallest guy in any room. Despite what everyone thought about him she loved him like a father.

Damien came up behind her and Lazzaro clapped him on the back. "I drove through your town Damien. I'm impressed with how much work you've done."

Hope couldn't help but notice how Damien puffed up a bit. The two of them had often disagreed about whether or not he should go back and claim his alpha status and fight for his pack. Damien felt betrayed by their people and Lazzaro had always dealt with betrayal and backstabbing but had felt it was his duty to lead the vampires on a different path than the destructive one they were on when his father and grandfather were kings.

When Violca stepped forward Hope noticed the look of affection that crossed his features. "Violca, you're looking stunning. Are you sure you wish to be mated to a guard when you could have a king?"

Chase's growl could be heard through the room but Violca simply laughed. She leaned up to kiss Lazzaro on the cheek and he dutifully bent down so she could reach. "I'm pretty taken with my dragon guard but I will remember your offer should he ever step out of line."

Chase came up and put an arm around Violca. Hope had a hard

time reading him but was hoping he knew that Lazzaro was simply teasing him. "I believe my wife and mate has made her choice."

Lazzaro gave him a cocky grin. "You can't blame a guy for noticing how lucky you are and hoping to find a mate of his own. At last you and Viktor turn me a little green with envy."

Viktor chuckled as he looked down at Aithne on his arm. Hope felt a small twinge of envy, eager for the time when she and Warrick would be that comfortable with each other. They were moving in the right direction, but she was a bit impatient.

"Lazzaro I would like you to meet Warrick," Hope said redirecting his attention to her mate who had come closer to her during their interaction. He was watching everything and looked a little amused by the banter.

Lazzaro turned and she noticed him quickly look Warrick over, sizing him up in a single look. Hope watched, as Warrick stood taller, the look on his face was remote as if he didn't care, which was not the same feeling she was getting through their connection. Lazzaro's eyes focused on the side of his neck and Hope realized that her bite mark on him was sticking partly out from under his shirt. The scar looked new and a little frenzied before he looked up at Warrick's face.

When he didn't smile, his scar looked more prominent. The pink puckering around the skin was mostly gone. By the time he awoke he had gained some weight and Violca had healed most of it. That first day after he was cleaned, it pulled on his lip and now his skin looked relaxed and the red angry looking skin that surrounded it was better.

"Let me know if you need any help finding your brother. It's unfortunate when your family are the ones you cannot trust," Lazzaro said as he nodded in Warrick's direction.

Warrick gave him a nod in return, reaching his hand out. "I wanted to thank you for taking care of Hope and making sure she was safe."

Lazzaro shook his hand. "Hope's mother made a plea I couldn't refuse," he said, looking at Violca.

Hope tilted her head wondering what that look was. She knew Violca had agreed to help him find a cure for the vampires who had been cursed to the night. Who would have believed playing with a witch's heart would have ever backfired? She used to tease him about all the girls she saw around him. Asking if he'd learned anything from his relatives -- women were dangerous.

After a few minutes of chit-chat, Hope looked up to see Eva sitting with Eryk on the couch. Hope had always seen Eva as the social butterfly, a bright, happy young woman, and she was surprised when, for a moment, she detected an air of sadness. When Eva looked up at her she blushed a bit before giving her a big bright smile. Hope almost believed she'd imagined that moment until she realized that for the first time, her big blue eyes didn't look to be full of mischief. She wondered what it was that could have possibly made her happy friend so melancholy.

Violca had left the room and walked back in with a big smile on her face. "Dinner is done. I think you guys will love it. The cooks really outdid themselves."

With that Chase joined her and everyone started walking out toward the door. Before she could hang back to walk with Eva, Warrick showed up at her side giving her a smile before offering her his arm. Lazzaro came up next to her and walked with them.

"Warrick, do you remember anything about the witches that helped keep you captive?" Lazzaro asked. Hope shook her head. Since finding those journals he had become obsessed with witches and gathering all the information he could. Black witches were very elusive.

Warrick shook his head, "They'd change how they look. I got the feeling that what I was seeing was a mask. There were times when I thought..."

Hope watched as he rubbed the back of his neck letting out a breath. "I don't think this is appropriate to talk about right now," she said giving Lazzaro a disapproving look that let him know she would not be okay with this conversation.

"You still get feisty when I mess with your new toys," Lazzaro said with a grin on his face that made her blush. Warrick looked uncomfortable but she could see him relax when the subject was dropped.

The table was set beautifully. Hope had rarely seen the staff when she was here. Violca had enjoyed cooking and except for when she was exhausted from healing Warrick she had been the one cooking dinners. For the first time she saw several staff members lined up to serve them the first course.

There were two women who delivered the food to them, while men carried around the trays. Hope smiled. They were older dragons, with streaks of grey hair and smile lines around their lips. They were dressed in black suits, freshly pressed. The only people who looked more formal were Lazzaro and Viktor.

When everyone had a glass of wine, and the staff had stepped back from serving the soup, Lazzaro cleared his throat and stood. Hope looked up to see him smiling down at her. "I would like to propose a toast," he said once he had everyone's attention. "To our newly fated couple who have proven that who the Fates have destined to be together, no one can keep apart."

13

Warrick raised his glass with everyone else, his eyes on Hope. A lovely shade of pink colored her cheeks as she looked up at Lazzaro giving him a bright smile before she looked across the table at Warrick. When she raised her glass to him, Warrick did the same, watching her as he took his own drink. When she lowered her glass, Warrick couldn't help but notice a drop of wine still on her lips. The wine was good. Rich, with a unique flavor. He smiled to himself as he imagined licking her lower lip to capture that taste along with her on his tongue.

Hope must have been reading his mind because she looked down biting her lip as she pushed her hair back behind her ear. Lazzaro chuckled as he sat down and Warrick realized that apparently his thoughts weren't as secret as he thought.

"Warrick, has there been any news yet on your brother's movement?" Lazzaro asked once the servants removed their appetizers and started bringing out the next course.

"No, so far we haven't been able to find a trace of him. Aithne put an alert on his accounts so we could find him but so far…" Warrick let his voice trail off.

Gabriel had disappeared without a trace ever since the night

Damien had arrived and challenged him. With everything being electronic these days Aithne was completely puzzled. "He must have someone helping him. Have you questioned all the old guards?" Lazzaro asked.

Damien nodded answering for him, "Aithne and Eva both questioned them. From what she was able to read we couldn't figure out who, if anyone, from the pack, was hiding him."

Lazzaro looked down toward Aithne who was sitting on the right of Viktor at the head of the table. Next to her was Eva who looked up, blushing slightly. Warrick sent her a small smile trying to ease her discomfort.

"Eva is young you shouldn't have her near wolves you think might betray you," Lazzaro said. His voice rougher than before, Warrick noticed the way Lazzaro's jaw had clenched and his hands looked like they might break the wine glass he was holding. But instead he set the glass on the table.

"We don't let her near them when we question..." Warrick started to explain when Lazzaro leveled him with a glance. The angry look on his face revealed the hunter that Lazzaro kept locked away. His wolf picked up on Lazzaro's challenge and he had to fight to keep control of his own animal instincts. The entire table had gone quiet and Hope cleared her throat distracting them both.

Warrick instantly relaxed when he saw the worried look on her face and he noticed that Lazzaro had visibly relaxed next to him.

"Sorry," Lazzaro said quietly.

When Hope shot Warrick a look he sighed. "I'm sorry too."

Hope smiled at Warrick shaking her head and he realized there was something about pleasing her that made him happy. He didn't think telling her would be the best thing. Silent now, not sure what to say, he thanked the woman who put a new plate in front of him. The smell was delicious and he looked over to see that Lazzaro had the same meal but his steak was a lot rarer. When he cut into it he smiled up at Aithne. "Nice and rare, thank you my fiery queen."

Aithne smirked. "I told the chef you wanted to hear it cry when you cut into it."

Lazzaro laughed and the little bit of tension that was left from the skirmish earlier was gone. Warrick listened to the conversations around him. Damien and Hope both asked him questions but for the most part he kept silent. He had spent so much time alone with Gabriel that he often felt overwhelmed when he was in a group of people. While in the basement the sounds he heard were usually of his brother having sex or fighting with someone. His brother loved to torture him. The only reason he didn't do those things in front of him was because he didn't want it to get out that there was someone locked in the basement that looked just like him.

After dessert he noticed Lazzaro follow Violca down the hall with Chase. Hope must have noticed too because she put her hand on his arm and smiled at him while also leading Warrick down the hall.

"Violca is helping Lazzaro figure out how to break the daylight curse," Hope said as they entered the living room. Scott left with Eryk right after dinner. Aithne and Eva were both talking together in the corner while Viktor and Damien poured themselves a scotch. When they saw him walk in Damien nodded and poured another glass.

"You guys are about to talk about boring stuff aren't you?" Hope asked, giving her brother a grin.

"I never talk about boring stuff," Damien replied.

Kassandra laughed as she walked into the room. "You shouldn't lie to your sister." She kissed him on the cheek and smiled. "You guys can talk about town stuff tomorrow. Tonight is just us celebrating how far everything's come."

Damien wrapped his arm around her and grinned. "True, tonight is about my baby sister finally getting her mate back, and the two of them together."

Hope blushed as she looked up at him. Warrick wrapped his arm around her and pulled her close. Every time they celebrated his return he only felt guilty about his brother Gabriel and everything that had happened. The death of both their parents, the last forty years of both packs trapped by his brother. Warrick had an endless supply of guilt too. His limp and the few scars were a constant reminder. Determined not to throw himself a pity party Warrick simply smiled when people brought it up.

After a bit Lazzaro finally entered the room. Damien noticed how his eyes scanned the room before he finally walked over to Hope and Warrick who were sitting on the couch talking to Eva. She was telling them about a few of the kids who had joined the college. Eva had been nice enough to help them get started and even tutored them in a few subjects. The second the door opened, Eva quit talking and watched Lazzaro.

"Pardon my interruption I just wanted to tell you all goodnight," Lazzaro said, smiling at Hope as she stood up. When he bent down to give her a hug Warrick noticed that he whispered something in her ear. Hope nodded and Warrick wondered what it was about.

Both he and Eva stood up. Warrick shook his hand and Lazzaro gave him a smile. "I'll be talking to you soon."

Lazzaro looked at Eva nodding before turning away. "Viktor, walk me out," he said as he headed toward the door. He winked at Aithne before adding, "You too of course."

Aithne rolled her eyes but let Viktor lead her out. Warrick chuckled as he looked to Hope. "Is he always like that."

Hope looked to Eva and then the three of them walked out. "For the most part. He actually kept himself reigned in."

Eva grinned as she sat down, "My sister told him he had to behave. When he was here for the wedding I kept waiting for Viktor and Chase to punch him for hitting on their mates."

Hope laughed. "That sounds more like him."

Warrick gave her a look and she shrugged. "Lazzaro has always loved pushing buttons. He says it keeps people on their toes. But he truly admires Violca and I think, despite his grumbling, he's happy how things worked out between Aithne and Viktor."

Eva looked over at the two and smiled. "Maybe the Fates used him to bring her into his life. A lot of good has come from that, including you two."

Hope smiled as she looked at him. Warrick felt his chest tighten and he wished he could be the man she deserved.

"You two ready to go home?" Damien asked as he walked up to them.

Thanking Eva, they told her goodbye. Walking with Viktor and Chase to the door the girls said goodbye to Aithne and Violca giving them a moment to talk alone. Viktor and Chase walked the four of them to the door.

"So Lazzaro offered to help with the guards at night. He has a few trusted vampires he'd like to send over but I wasn't sure how your people, or mine, would react. Mine are still getting used to having Lazzaro show up at night," Viktor told him as they approached the front door.

"I agree. They're extremely grateful for him saving us as children but they're not sure about all vampires," Damien said.

"I think it sounds like a good idea but we'd need to approach it carefully," Warrick said putting his two cents in. He didn't really care how uncomfortable they were, as long as Hope was safe. He mated with Hope and he knew firsthand his brother could be spiteful.

"Let's meet up tomorrow for lunch and come up with some thoughts on how to use them to our advantage. I don't want to spook anyone. Everyone is already on edge and I don't want vampires in the backyard to be the tipping point," Viktor said just before the women joined them.

Hope and Kassandra gave them both a look that said they both planned on being there. Before Aithne cleared her throat, "This sounds like it might need a woman's touch. Why don't we all meet up tomorrow for lunch."

Viktor chuckled bowing his head to his wife, "We know better than to exclude any of you from these conversations."

Damien laughed and when Kassandra gave him a look he shook his head, "Nice to see that I'm not the only one whose wife looks good wearing the pants."

Aithne and Kassandra both laughed and Hope just grinned shaking her head. As they walked outside they said their final goodbyes to Viktor and Aithne, agreeing to meet up tomorrow. Warrick helped Hope in the back of the truck, closing the door once she'd put on her seatbelt.

On the drive back, Warrick listened to them speak about dinner, just commenting when something was directed at him. They picked up their car at Kassandra's place and headed home together. "Did you enjoy your dinner?" Hope asked.

"It was good. The conversations were interesting. Lazzaro seems very interested in the witches," Warrick said thinking about how protective Lazzaro was of Eva when he mentioned bringing her in for questioning, the wolves, and his interest in the black witches that had kept him tied up.

"He's been interested in witches since he found the journals of one of his ancestors. He'd been tracking down books of spells ever since I can remember. He read them all and has been sending them to Violca," Hope said with a shrug.

Warrick thought about how he hadn't seen the sun in forty years and he could understand why Lazzaro was trying so hard to let his people back into the light. The day he woke up and felt the sun on his face...Warrick would never forget that feeling, nor take it for granted.

"Is he always so protective of them?" Warrick asked remembering that spark of anger while they were talking about Eva helping with interrogations tonight.

Hope shrugged her shoulders, quiet for a moment before finally replying, "When it comes to them he is pretty protective. They're still just learning to use their magic. But I've never seen him act that way."

Warrick nodded as they pulled up to the house. When they got out, Warrick opened the gate and put his hand on her lower back leading her up to the house. There was something amazing about coming home, knowing that he would be sleeping with her, holding her, claiming her as his.

Hope looked over her shoulder as they stepped into the house. A small blush on her cheeks and he knew she was thinking the same thing he was. "Are you ready to go to bed?"

He nodded and felt her slide her hand into his as she led him upstairs. He looked her over from the back as he followed her long hair down her back to the curve of her ass. Each step she took caused those muscles to flex and he bit back a moan. His eyes roamed farther down to her legs. She was built for him. The Fates had decided the moment she was born she was to be his. His to protect and to keep safe. So far he had failed miserably but now he had a second chance to keep her safe.

Once in the room Hope went to turn on the light and he stopped her hand. When she looked up at him, Warrick shook his head. Reaching up he carefully undid the clasp for the necklace he'd given her earlier. He put it on top of the dresser near the door as he gently guided her to the bed.

When she sat and he kneeled before her reaching down to undo the heels she'd worn to dinner. Warrick smiled as he noticed that the red nail polish on her toenails matched her fingernails. Unbuckling the clasp, he carefully removed her shoes, placing them nicely on the side of the bed. Warrick noticed how her feet were so much smaller than his as he slowly began to massage the bottom of one foot, working his hand up to her ankle before gently taking off the other.

Hope made a small sigh as his hand took care to rub her heel. Warrick looked up to see her watching him. Her eyes half closed, a small smile playing on her lips. "That feels wonderful."

He smiled and reached out a hand to help her stand. "Your feet are cute," he said as he undid her pants. He noticed how she opened her mouth to say something, but snapped it closed when his hand brushed her stomach to undo her zipper. With his hands on both sides of her hips he slowly rolled off her jeans, revealing her legs.

Warrick held up one leg to remove first one, then the other, from her pants. Next came her blouse. Warrick took it off carefully before tossing it to the side with her black jeans. Hope stood before him clad only in a black lace bra and a pair of panties that hinted at treasures yet to be unwrapped.

"Beautiful," he whispered as he brushed her cheek with a finger.

Warrick watched transfixed as she closed her eyes before tilting her head, caressing his finger with her cheek. Her red lips parted just slightly. Warrick gave in to the temptation and dipped his head to kiss her. It was meant to be a soft kiss but when her tongue touched his, Warrick felt himself growl as his hand slid to the back of her neck angling her face up for a long deep kiss.

Warrick felt Hope put her hand on his chest. Her fingers curling into his shirt as she held him tight and their tongues dueled. He swallowed her moan as her mouth parted more and her tongue slid deep into his mouth. She tasted of the wine from dinner. He sucked on her tongue as his free hand slid around her waist pulling her closer.

Hope's hand began to move on his chest and he smiled against her lips when he realized she was pulling his shirt from his jeans. As she pulled his shirt up and over his head she broke the kiss and he watched as she tossed it somewhere behind him.

He watched as she bit her lip. Her fingers traveling down his chest until they reached the top of his pants. Hope looked up at him, her eyes meeting his before she slowly undid his belt. When she paused he looked at her and noticed how she bit her lower lip. Warrick cupped her cheeks holding her still as he brushed his lips back and forth against hers.

He heard her soft sigh as she leaned forward, her nipples pushing against his chest causing him to moan. "Warrick," she said softly, causing him to pull back and look at her. "I can feel your uncertainty about me…with our connection."

Warrick sighed feeling like a jerk for making her feel unsure about anything. "It's not you Hope. The uncertainty comes from me," he said taking a deep breath, "I just want to make sure you're happy."

Hope nodded and her fingers began to undo his jeans. The sound of the zipper was loud in the very quiet room. Warrick toed off his shoes and kicked them aside. "Did I seem like I was unhappy after what we did last night?"

Warrick closed his eyes as she slowly pulled down his jeans. He remembered last night, every vivid moment, including her crying out in pleasure. His cock was instantly hard and he shook his head. "No. Unhappy was the furthest from what you seemed."

Hope smiled as she stepped closer to him. Both of them naked except for their underwear, leaving not much of a barrier. "I would like to think that I also pleased you last night."

Her amber eyes looked into his and he smiled down at her as he traced a line from her jaw down her neck until he reached the bite mark on her skin. His fingers traced the mark. He loved the way she shivered against him, sucking in a small breath. "You pleased me more than I could have imagined."

The smile she gave him was breathtaking. Then she brought herself up on her tippy toes, pressing herself firmly against him and said, "Make me happy again Warrick."

14

Hope curled up on Warrick's chest and woke up with a smile on her lips as she heard him snoring softly. She couldn't help but feel all happy and tingly and the fact that he was sleeping so soundly made her feel even better. After they'd made love -- twice -- he'd pulled her close, drifted off to sleep, and slept straight through the night.

Hope stretched a bit and felt him tighten his arms around her. The sound of birds outside the window let her know they had slept in later than normal and she was totally okay with that. She looked out the window to see the light just starting to creep in as a light breeze caused the curtains to move slightly.

A low growl rumbled in Warrick's chest and she felt his arm tighten almost painfully around her waist. Before she could protest, she felt him sit straight up in bed, his eyes wide as he looked around the room.

"Gabriel," she heard him growl out as he forced her to sit up with him.

"Warrick?" Hope said. Her squirming in his arms caused him to look down at her and release his hold.

Hope looked around trying to figure out what had his attention when he shot from the bed to the window. He pulled back the curtains looking out the open window and into the yard. She pulled the blankets up to cover herself while watching him. "Warrick is everything okay?"

He looked back toward her and she saw his shoulders sag. "I thought I smelled Gabriel. Felt him near us."

She stared at him, her head swimming with the idea of Gabriel coming after him. As he put on his pants, she got up from the bed trying to stop him. "You can't go out there."

Warrick zipped up his pants, "I have to. What if he's still out there just waiting for you to be alone?" he asked as he left the room. She heard him jogging down the stairs and Hope felt a surge of panic.

She shook her head, got out of bed, and grabbed a pair of yoga pants plus a t-shirt she found in the top drawer. Gabriel was never going to hurt Warrick or anyone else she loved, ever again. Slipping on her tennis shoes she quickly ran form the room to make her way down the stairs just in time to see the back-door close.

That nagging feeling of something wrong spurred her to move fast as she went outside. Hope could have followed his scent easily, but once he'd bitten her it was amazing how instinct took over to find her mate.

She took off in a light jog following him. The path he took through town quickly led back to the mountains and she frowned when she saw him standing at a trail. She realized that he hadn't put on any shoes or even a shirt. Hope knew she should be happy he even remembered to put pants on before he took off from the house.

"His scent disappears right here," Warrick said as he ran his fingers through his hair in frustration.

Hope stepped closer to him putting her hand on his arm. "Let's go home and call Damien. We can set up groups to go searching for him."

"I should––" Warrick started to say before she cut him off.

"Be home with me putting more clothes on. You're not going after him by yourself."

Hope realized that she sounded harsher than she'd meant to. She was worried about him. His brother had tortured him for years and she was afraid of what would happen if Gabriel managed to capture him again. Since everything was out in the open, would he kill him this time? A small whimper escaped her. She didn't even realize she had made a sound until Warrick stood before her holding her hand.

"Are you okay?" Warrick asked with concern in his voice.

Hope nodded, smiling at him. "Let's just go home. Please?"

He nodded and she saw him looking back over his shoulder at the path. She knew he wanted to go and find his brother and she was relieved when he finally started walking with her, back the way they had come.

"Warrick, promise me you won't go after your brother by yourself?" Hope asked watching his face. His jaw had hardened and she could feel the war within him.

"My brother will never catch me off guard again, Hope." His voice was hard and she wondered what she had said to make him mad. She waited for him to promise, and when none came she sighed and kept walking with him. Gabriel had kept them apart for years and she now worried that he would separate them again.

They didn't say a word the entire way home. That wall that was between them seemed to grow bigger with each step. The only thing that kept Hope from thinking all was lost was that Warrick kept a tight hold of her hand. Once inside, Hope went into the kitchen and found her cell phone to call her brother. It was a short call once she told him that Warrick had smelled Gabriel. Damien growled, telling her to lock the doors and he would be right over. Hope ignored his orders and just waited for him to show up.

While she made coffee, Warrick went upstairs. She heard him walking around and she sighed, feeling lost. It felt like forever but, if she had to guess, her brother was there in less than twenty minutes. When he came in he marched into the kitchen and gave her a dirty look. "I told you to lock the door."

Hope, handing him a cup of coffee, heard Warrick coming down the stairs. She said, "Well I would have but I also knew you'd have guards outside our house within a few minutes and I didn't want to have to go and let you in and have you yell at me for unlocking the door without making sure it was clear."

Kassandra laughed as she walked into the kitchen. Hope had made everyone a cup of coffee. Kassandra took hers and gave Hope a kiss on the cheek. Handing Warrick his cup, Hope noticed he was looking at Damien leaning a hip against the counter,

"I can protect her from my brother," Warrick said.

Damien raised an eyebrow. "I don't doubt you can. But since he's not dead yet I'm going to make sure your brother doesn't get a chance to hurt her... or you."

"You should've killed him," Warrick said between gritted teeth.

Hope saw her brother nod. She knew Damien well enough to know he regretted not killing Gabriel after they had figured everything out. Killing a shifter was a big deal. At first she was glad he didn't kill him, but after all they'd learned, it might have been better.

The words hung in the air and no one said anything for a few minutes. Everyone looked lost in their own thoughts as a knock sounded at the door. Warrick and Damien both walked towards it, leaving the girls to follow.

"We have three different groups right now checking out the trails. All of them have been staying on coms and no one has found any trace of him," stated the guard at the door.

Hope recognized the wolf. His name was Matthew and he was one of the men who had helped take care of the young and the elderly as they made their transition. He was to make sure they had everything, and overall, he was very helpful. He was older and she had heard that his wife had died during childbirth while he was being forced to fight. Chase had noticed him too, when they were training, and had pointed him out to Damien, who made him one of the top guards.

"Thank you Matt. Keep us posted if anything changes. Have them look for another hour, and I want you to change the patrol, adding two more guys per patrol. Also, reach out to Chase and have him add some of the dragons as well," Damien said.

"We can protect our own," Matthew said, sounding offended. "Gabriel will not be slipping past us a second time."

Damien gave him a nod. "We don't doubt you or our people at all. But the same thing that hides us from the outside world can be our weakness. There're mountains and miles and miles of trails. There's a lot of ground to cover. We don't need them in town but it would be helpful to have them be on the lookout on the trails behind their homes."

Hope watched the guard's face as he nodded. He no longer looked offended as he realized that the request was not a lack of faith in them but the fact that they only had so many trained men. Besides the trails that ran along the mountains, there were acres of land and caves that one could easily hide in.

"Gabriel is tricky and uses magic. If you smell something coppery or feel something sticky, let us know. When the witch sisters came to the town to help us move they'd all felt sick to their stomach. Chase took them home almost immediately. We should tell them as well," Damien announced and Warrick nodded.

Warrick patted Matthew on the back. "Thank you for all your help."

Matthew nodded and Hope smiled realizing that was Warrick's way of making him feel better. Gabriel would never be able to take over the packs again but that didn't mean he couldn't try to attack them. They worried about the previous guards. The few that seemed the most resistant to losing their status over the pack members were kicked out, or they'd left on their own as soon as they were given the chance. Those also seemed to be the ones who were the cruelest. Everyone knew the threat Gabriel made on Hope's life while he had kept Warrick chained up. As sister to one alpha, and mate to the other, both packs kept an eye on her. Hope had noticed a long time ago that she was usually surrounded by a group of females when she was helping around town. There was also a guard almost always near her. She asked her brother once if it was his doing and he shook his head saying he knew better than to try and always watch her. Hope knew that it was Warrick who had set that up even though she'd never talked to him about it.

Warrick closed the door and looked around the room, when his eyes fell on hers he sighed, running a hand through his hair. There was an immense amount of guilt coming off him and she felt like Gabriel was once again ruining her life and happiness. Unable to help herself she stomped her foot. "He's not going to win."

Kassandra smiled and Hope realized she sounded like a little kid. "No, he's not," she said agreeing, before looking at the two men in the room who were both frowning at them. "You two are not allowed to turn into our jailers."

The look Warrick and Damien gave the girls said they planned to argue. "If Gabriel gets his hands on either of you —"

"My brother has been trying to kill you since you were barely able to walk," Warrick said while taking a step toward her.

Kassandra spoke before Hope could come up with a reply. "I will start training with Hope on how to fight in her human form," she said before looking at Warrick. "You two will train in wolf form together. That way if he comes, she is better prepared to defend herself and you get some more practice too."

Warrick looked like he wanted to argue. Hope stood as tall as she could next to Kassandra pretending not to be afraid. She wasn't so much worried about Gabriel as she was about how he would affect her very fragile relationship with her mate.

"Your brother already stole the first part of my life from me. He is not taking anything else," Hope said, wondering if he understood her meaning.

Warrick finally nodded before saying. "Just please, don't go anywhere alone and make sure one of us knows where you're going. At least if you're with someone else then Gabriel will have to either take both of you or leave a witness."

Hope gave him a look before saying, "Only if you promise to do the same. He wants you too."

Damien nodded, "That would be a good idea. I know it's not what either one of you want to do, but it'll be easier for us to figure out where to look and backtrack if we know where you are and who you're with."

Everyone was quiet, sipping their coffee, lost in their own thoughts for a bit. Kassandra had gone to stand near Damien who instantly reached out to put an arm around her and pull her close. She rested her head on his shoulder. Kassandra and Damien were equal in every way. She was a warrior who would always fight by his side.

Hope glanced at Warrick, wondering how she complimented him. She had been sheltered for most of her life where he had been tortured by his brother for most of his. Kept hostage in the dark, their tentative link used to keep everyone under control. Even now, Gabriel was using their bond to try and keep the two of them apart. Warrick and Hope sat next to each other on the couch. Not touching but close enough to feel each other's heat.

"We have lunch plans with Aithne and Viktor, why don't we go home and get ready. After lunch, Hope, I will take you with me for a small training session," Kassandra stated looking at her.

"Okay. We'll meet up with you guys at your place," Hope said in agreement.

Everyone agreed and Damien and Kassandra left. Damien stopped in the doorway and gave Hope a big hug before whispering orders to lock all the doors and keep an eye on Warrick. Hope smiled at that. He was the one person who truly understood how much it had hurt thinking that her mate had betrayed her for all those years.

After everyone left, Hope looked to Warrick. She didn't want him ruining the connection they had started. A mischievous idea formed in her head and she took his hand, leading him up the stairs. "Where are we going?" She heard him ask hesitantly as he obediently followed her.

"I'm taking a shower and you're going to keep an eye on me by joining me."

15

Warrick wanted to argue with Hope telling her that he had stuff to do. That argument didn't stay in his head very long as he watched her walk up the stairs. Her hips swayed gently and the pants she wore hugged her curves in just a way that he decided she should not wear those in public. Hope took him to the master bathroom and closed the door behind them.

It didn't take her long to shed her clothes. Without a word, she started the water for the shower. The master bathroom was much bigger than the other bathrooms. Hope had designed it herself and it had a big tub that stood by itself and a shower stall built for two with two showerheads, one on either side.

Once he was naked Hope opened the glass door of the shower and stepped inside. Expecting him to follow, she left the door open without a glance back. Not wanting to disappoint her he stepped in and closed the door.

Warrick let the water hit his back as he watched Hope. Her head tilted back, her back arched causing her breasts to tilt up. He noticed how her pink nipples had already hardened. All he could do was watch as a drop of water ran down between the valley of her breasts and his eyes followed it downward. The drop went down her flat belly and into her belly button.

Feeling her eyes on him, he looked up to see Hope watching. The feelings coming from her were mixed. He could feel her desire and something else-- he had hurt her. Warrick didn't understand what he'd done to upset her so he stepped forward and cupped her cheek.

The only sound was the water hitting them. Hope turned her cheek and nuzzled his hand, sighing softly.

"You left me," Hope finally whispered before opening her eyes and looking at him.

Warrick opened his mouth to say something to explain. He didn't think she would understand his need to protect her from Gabriel. His brother was cruel and she was everything beautiful and right in the world. Warrick's thumb traced the line of her cheekbone. "I did."

Hope put her hands on his chest and he watched as her eyes searched his. "I'm your mate Warrick. The Fates picked me to fight by your side. You're not alone and I'm no longer a four year old girl who can't defend herself."

He wanted to argue. Tell her that it would always be his job to protect her. There were so many things he could have said, but instead he gave in to temptation and bent down to kiss her upturned lips. As he brushed his lips back and forth across hers he felt her stiffen for a moment before she sighed and slid her arms around his neck.

The water hit his back as they stood in the shower and he slid his hand from her jaw to the back of her neck. With his free hand wrapped around her waist, he pulled her close to him. Turning her slightly, he pushed her against the wall of the shower. This new position caused the water to hit them from both sides.

With a moan, he thrust into her mouth then he felt her suck on his tongue. His hands slid from her hips, up her flat stomach, which quivered under his touch, until he cupped her breasts. He broke the kiss and trailed his lips down her jaw to her neck. Then, he kissed and nibbled his way down as his thumb continued to slide back and forth across her nipple.

"Warrick," Hope said, her back arched as if she were offering him her tempting breasts. "We're still going to talk about what you did today."

He nodded as he finally brought his face down to her breast and flicked her nipple with his tongue collecting a drop of water that hung off it. He couldn't help but smile at the sound that escaped her. As her back arched, he watched her nipple pebble a little more.

"Did you bring me in here to talk, Hope?" Warrick asked as he brought his attention to her other breast, licking that nipple, collecting the water before sucking it into his mouth.

Hope's hand slid into his hair and he felt her hold him close. "You can't walk away if you're wet and naked."

For a second he was confused by what she was saying, so instead he concentrated on her breast. He smiled against her as his tongue came out and flicked her nipple. "You are a clever little minx."

Hope tugged his hair back a bit forcing him to look up at her. Desire was plain to read on her face. Her cheeks were flushed, her amber eyes looked dark and her pupils had dilated in need. He noticed the way she bit her lower lip and could see her struggling with the needs of her body and her desire to talk to him.

"Later," Warrick said keeping his eyes locked with hers until she nodded.

His need to touch her, make sure that she was okay, was over-riding everything else. He kissed her breast before lowering himself to his knees, kissing his way down her body. Warrick kissed her stomach as her body arched to him. With her head and shoulders against the wall of the shower, he looked up and it was like the steam of the shower formed a cloud, surrounding her in a mist. She looked like a vision from one of his dreams. Her eyes were half closed, with a look of desire and need on her face.

He had spent years dreaming about her. Some nights he dreamt of making love to her, being able to kiss every inch of her body. The older he got the more vivid his dreams got. His tongue followed a drop of water that ran down the side of her stomach curving along her delicate hipbone. When her hips rolled up he growled softly, his head even with the soft blonde curls that hid her from him. Curious if she tasted as good as she smelled he dipped his head more as his tongue came out and licked her wet folds.

Hope gasped above him, the hands holding his hair tightened and her hips rocked higher, her legs parted just enough to give him more room. Warrick wanted to see more of her, to see all of her beautiful secrets so he reached out with a hand and brought her leg to his shoulder causing her to open more for him.

He had dreamt of seeing her this way. Warrick heard a small whimper and looked up to see her biting her lower lip as she looked down at him. She looked beautiful and vulnerable.

"Beautiful," he whispered before leaning forward and licking up her slit again, his eyes on her the whole time. Her lips parted and her head went back. He noticed that her eyes closed as her hips bucked up to meet his mouth.

Feeling a surge of masculine pride he licked her again, this time his tongue stopping at her clit. Curious about the little nub, he flicked it with his tongue. When he felt her leg on his shoulder tighten pulling him closer he closed his mouth around it and sucked gently.

Warrick had never been more aware of everything than he was right now. The water hitting him on the top of his head as he knelt between her legs, worshipping her body. Proving to him that his brother had not won and that she was okay.

With Hope against the wall between the two showerheads he began to lap at her in earnest as the water cascaded down her body. His cock throbbed in need every time she whimpered or pulled on his hair letting him know when she liked something.

Unable to hold back any longer, Warrick stood up. He wrapped her leg around his hip and he entered her with one long hard thrust. Hope's hip eagerly came up to meet his and he kissed her hard, swallowing her moan. Warrick wanted to go slow but when her hands slid around his back to grip his ass tight and she sucked on his tongue, whatever control he had, snapped.

His hips moved faster, harder, her body contracting tight around him increasing his pleasure. Warrick broke the kiss, putting his forehead against hers as he fought to catch his breath.

"Warrick," Hope panted and he felt her leg shake against his.

Without missing a beat Warrick gripped her ass to hold her up as she buried her head in his neck. Her mouth finding her mark on him, she bit hard muffling her cry of pleasure. The intense feeling of pleasure and pain sent him over the edge and instinct took over as he sunk his teeth into his mark on her while he thrust his cock deep inside her.

They stood that way for a while, him holding her leg on his hip with his other hand still holding her ass as the water hit their bodies. Warrick felt his cock soften and slip from her core. Hope's soft whimper made him smile as he licked his mark on her shoulder. He could feel her doing the same and he nipped at her gently.

Warrick pulled back and looked down at her. He released her leg, waiting for her to get her footing before he released her and cupped her cheek. He watched as she turned her head and nuzzled his hand. "Amazing."

Hope blushed softly and he turned to her so he could wash her. Her back to the water he enjoyed the gentle massage of the opposite shower head as he soaped up his hands. Starting with her back, his hands caressed every inch of her. He paused when he got to her ass, cupping it before massaging her.

Going down to his knees he massaged the back of her thighs with his soapy hands before tapping her so she could turn around. Warrick massaged each foot as he washed them slowly sliding back up her thighs. When he got to the juncture between her thighs he tenderly washed her. She moaned and he looked up to see her eyes closed. Warrick kissed her belly button before moving up. He carefully massaged her breasts. Her back arched up and he watched her face as he slowly moved from her breasts to her arms.

Hope was beautiful; she was everything he had dreamed of. She responded to his touch and was giving in her passion. When he finished she offered to wash him. Kissing her on the nose he smiled.

"No, let me take care of that while you get ready. We're probably expected soon for lunch."

With a smile she kissed him. "Okay. Hurry though. I don't want to explain why you're late."

16

Hope took her time getting dressed and doing her hair. Warrick was right, by the time she got done blow-drying her hair it was almost time to leave. She slipped on a pair of jeans and a blouse. When Warrick came out of his room dressed, she smiled thinking that tomorrow she would move his clothes over. Maybe they would also go out and buy him new clothes. He only had a handful of things and she wanted to change that.

"Ready to go?" Hope asked as she slipped on a pair of tennis shoes.

Warrick nodded, as he looked her over. "Yeah, I just received a text from your brother. Apparently, we're all just meeting over at Kassandra's."

"It's going to be nice when they move in next door and we no longer have to drive over there," Hope said as they started down the stairs. She watched as Warrick checked the back door before they headed out the front. Warrick locked up and she noticed how he checked everything before he led them out the door.

Hope hadn't been thinking when she led him to the shower earlier. She just had a desire to clean herself, thinking after that Gabriel might have been listening to them...or possibly watching them. She also needed Warrick to be close. Pulling him into the shower seemed the best way to take care of both of those options. When he kissed her she realized they would not be talking, but he felt so good she couldn't stop herself from melting into him.

They drove together in silence. Hope kept looking at him out of the corner of her eye, noticing how he sat rigid. He kept glancing out the window to make sure they weren't being followed. She bit back a sigh, her shoulders sagging a bit thinking, *that was a short honeymoon period*. Gabriel seemed to be consistently messing up her life.

When they pulled up, she saw that Viktor's SUV was already parked in the driveway. She and Warrick walked up together and before they could knock, Damien opened the door. She noticed the small worry lines around his eyes and lips. Being that they were twins they were close, but since they'd lost their parents at such a young age, the two of them had become inseparable.

"Has there been any sign of him?" Warrick asked as the two of them came into the house.

"No traces of him anywhere. Your brother is like a fucking ghost," Damien said and Hope noticed how he clenched his fists at his sides.

Kassandra came in with Aithne, both of them carrying a tray of food. Kassandra put hers down first and came up behind Damien putting her hand on his back. Hope watched as her brother visibly relaxed, but then she looked away feeling as if she were intruding on a private moment between the two. When she looked up at Warrick she noticed how he tensed with the mention of his brother. Not sure if he would welcome her touch in comfort she sighed, her shoulders sagging.

Viktor came in from the kitchen, a drink in his hand, and gave her a wink before putting his arm around Aithne. "We'll find him. No one can hide forever. We just need to figure out who is helping him and how."

Hope felt Warrick move in behind her and put his hand on her back leading her to the loveseat. "Besides the witches I never really saw him interact with anyone," Warrick said as he sat down next to her.

Viktor sat on the chair across from them while Kassandra and Damien took the couch. Aithne stood behind Viktor her hand on his shoulder as she watched them. "Do you remember anything about the witches who helped your brother?" Aithne asked.

Warrick tried to piece together his memories of the witches. Most times there was just one, but on rare occasions, four of them showed up. At first glance they were beautiful. He thought they were all young but one day he saw one in the mirror's reflection and realized what he saw was just a glamor spell hiding what was underneath. Warrick kept his voice low as he started to tell them what he could remember. "I believe they were either cousins or sisters. They used a glamor spell to hide how they looked but when you see them in a reflection they're older and scarred."

Aithne listened to him intently. After a few minutes she asked, "Did they use any names or did you see any tattoos?"

Warrick closed his eyes thinking about it. There was something, a memory teasing him. As he tried to hold onto it, he began to feel like he was suffocating. As his body tensed up he began to feel like he was back there again. Tied up. A knife slicing into his side as they tried to drain him. Before he could start panicking he felt Hope. Her scent, her light touch on his arm, the feel of her and her wolf through their mated connection.

"One. I remember one name Natasia. She had a tattoo on her arm, it looked like a bird with long feathers that were tied into a Celtic knot. I felt like she was their leader," Warrick said.

Warrick felt Hope squeezing his hand. Her touch kept him from freaking out as he tried to remember the others. "Whenever they walked in the room it was like the entire room felt oppressive, dark." He opened his eyes looking at Viktor. "When Violca and her sisters are around you can feel the good in them. It is in the air and makes you feel drawn to them, like you want to protect them. These witches made the animal in me want to come out fight."

Viktor nodded and he noticed how everyone looked at Aithne. Warrick often forgot that she was the oldest one of everyone. Given immortality by a Celtic Goddess, her mother was talked about in history books. Warrick wondered what people would do if they found out that Boudicca actually still lived and that her youngest daughter became an assassin before becoming the mate of the Dragon King.

"There were rumors of witches that made up a dark coven. They used the power of other witches and other supernaturals to feed their own. The first time I heard about them they'd kidnapped a bunch of children. They were trying to steal their youth," Aithne said with a small shudder.

"How come I have never heard of them before?" Kassandra asked.

"They were a small group. I thought I… I thought I'd killed them all," Aithne said looking down at her hands.

Warrick could feel her discomfort as she admitted to killing them. To be honest, he doubted he would feel that guilt if he killed anyone trying to kill children, Viktor grabbed her hand and pulled her onto his lap. He had often watched his parents comfort each other with just a touch and for the first time he totally understood.

When Warrick glanced at Hope he couldn't help but notice how she looked sad. He gave her a smile and squeezed her hand. She smiled back at him and realized she was sad for him. It had been so long since someone had cared about him that he'd forgotten what that felt like.

"Do you think they could help my brother hide?" Warrick asked Aithne.

"If it's the same group, they could, but they would have to be getting something out of it. From what I saw, this coven did nothing that didn't first help themselves."

"How is it they aren't leaving a scent of magic behind?" Kassandra asked, wrinkling her nose.

Warrick wondered the same thing. He hadn't detected that acidic smell like he did when they came around, or when the one slowly covered the town they used to live in.

"They might be using a cloaking spell. It'd be similar to how

Kassandra's ability works," Aithne said making a point to look around at each of them before she continued. "Which means he intentionally made sure you were aware of him today and wanted you to follow him."

Hope tensed up next to him. He could feel her hand tighten on his and knew that she was starting to worry. If this were a trap, was it to get him…or Hope? Gabriel had often threatened that he would hurt Hope. Taking an almost perverse pleasure in teasing Warrick with what he would do to her. Warrick held on for so long because Gabriel had said the second he died he would find Hope and she would take his spot.

"You're going to need to resist the urge to follow him next time," Damien said as he gave Warrick a hard look. "You running after him puts both you and my sister in danger."

"We can't be under guard all day every day Damien," Hope said, her anger directed at her brother. "We've been hiding long enough. I want to live my life."

"The keyword there is 'live' my dear sister and if I think locking you in a tower for a few weeks while we hunt him down is what needs to happen, then that is exactly what I will do," Damien said.

Warrick growled low in the back of his throat. Damien might be his equal but Hope was his mate. Damien growled back at him, his lips pulling back as his fangs started to descend. "No one will ever lock her away." Warrick said firmly

Kassandra put her hand on Damien's thigh. "Damien would never lock up Hope."

He heard Hope snort next to him. "I'd never allow him too. What I do is up to me. Gabriel doesn't get to dictate my life anymore."

Warrick kept his mouth shut. If he knew his brother, locking her up would be the nicest thing he would do to her. Gabriel had boasted for years about how he would rape her and torture her. These threats came, mostly, when he seemed to want to hurt Warrick the most but, after all that had happened, he believed his brother would follow through just to mess with him.

"No one is getting locked up, but unless you two are at your house you'll have someone with you. No going off alone and we'll be doubling the patrolling guards. In both towns and in the mountains," Aithne said giving them a look that let them know she would not take no for an answer. "I also think Damien and Kassandra should move into the house next to you as soon as possible."

Kassandra was the first to nod. Damien took a moment before nodding. With everything temporarily settled, Kassandra piped up, "Now that's all settled. I believe we should eat the lunch that Aithne brought over for us."

17

The next few days fell into a routine. Kassandra picked Hope up every morning and trained with her until she was exhausted. Kassandra was fierce and despite her fast healing, Hope was covered in bruises. Today Kassandra pushed her so hard all she could do was soak in a hot tub with the jets on.

She had put head back as the water soothed her muscles when she heard Warrick come home. He had been helping Damien finish up the final touches on the house next door in preparation for them to move in. Tomorrow they would start painting. Damien thought they would be moving in by the end of the week.

She had gotten used to the sound of his footsteps. His slight limp had gotten better every day. Tomorrow Warrick would start sparring with her in wolf form, which meant Kassandra was going to give her the day off. Hope listened as their bedroom door opened. They had made love every night. With the threat of his brother hanging over them Warrick had gotten fierce in taking her. Touching every inch of her, kissing each bruise, refusing to let her do anything but enjoy his touch until finally when she was begging for him, he would make love to her.

She heard his footsteps right outside the bathroom door. When he finally turned the handle and entered, she couldn't help but smile as she lay back with her eyes closed. After a moment of silence she opened her eyes and saw him looking at her. He was covered in a light dust from sanding, making his hair look a little lighter. His normally light eyes were dark as he looked down at her in the water.

"Are you going to join me?" she asked a slow smile curving her lips.

Warrick bent his arms down caging her in as he gripped the sides of the tub. His lips brushed hers, feather light, and she sighed happily. "Even covered in bruises you look beautiful. I should talk to Kassandra later and tell her to lighten up."

Hope smiled, shaking her head. "I'm fine. Nothing a long hot bath won't fix."

Warrick smiled and she gasped as he reached into the water sprinkling her face with a tiny bit of water, playfully. Hope grinned while reaching up to grab his shirt then pulled him down to her. Having caught him off guard, his hand slipped off the side and he fell into the tub and on top of her.

The sound of the water sloshing over the side and her laughter echoed through the bathroom. She quit laughing and noticed he hadn't made a sound. She started to worry that he didn't find the humor in what she'd done. When he finally pulled back to look at her she noticed the serious set of his jaw.

"Warrick –– I" she started to say when he growled.

"You think you're funny, huh?"

Not sure what to do she bit her lower lip when he suddenly grinned at her and started tickling her sides. "I'll show you funny," he said as she laughed under him, her body twisting and turning under his and the water sloshing over the sides.

When he finally stopped she was leaning against his side, her wet naked body draped over his. His fully clothed body was completely submerged in the water. These moments with him being relaxed were few and far between since Gabriel showed up. When she looked up at him she saw a smile on his lips but as he looked down he frowned slightly. "I didn't hurt you, did I?"

Hope shook her head, "No you didn't hurt me. Still tender from Kassandra throwing me around but that's about it."

"Are you sure you want to practice fighting as your wolf tomorrow night?" Warrick asked as his hand began to stroke up and down her back.

"I'm sure," Hope said. She relaxed under the warm water and his gentle caress. "I am not sparring with Kassandra tomorrow and these bruises should be pretty much healed." Giving him a big grin she looked up and he raised an eyebrow back at her. "Why? Are you scared I'll beat you?"

Warrick grinned and bent down to kiss her nose. "I have no doubt you will, but I just wanted to make sure you wanted to. Some of these bruises your brother's mate has given you look angry."

Hope looked down at her thighs. On the side of her right thigh was a huge bruise that did indeed look angry. It was blue and black in places and when she'd touched it earlier she had winced. Despite how ugly it looked today, she knew by the morning it would be gone. Besides a very long life where she aged slowly, their ability to heal quickly was probably her second favorite perk. It was first when she was younger and clumsy. She had thought she would outgrow being clumsy before working with Kassandra. Based on these bruises she wasn't as coordinated as she thought she was.

"They will heal soon," she said, simply leaning up and kissing him. She liked this side of him. The side that was playful and just a little worried about her.

When she smiled against his lips he nodded toward some of the small wood chips that were floating in the tub. "I've ruined your bath."

Hope continued to brush her lips back and forth against his. "I think the only way that would've been better is if you were naked... you're by far wearing too many clothes."

Warrick chuckled and lightly smacked her ass as he gave her a big kiss. With her hands holding his shirt, she felt herself melt into him. He had been training her to respond to him the last few days and her body was eager to see where this playfulness would go. "I'm sorry I ruined your bath but I have to change and head out. One of the guards is celebrating his anniversary and I'm taking over for him until his replacement can come."

Once he was out, she started to get out of the tub only to have him reach down and pick her up. Wrapping her in a big towel, he kissed her nose as he let out the water. He rinsed the tub out and started to fill it again. "You, my dear Hope, should take another bath and relax. I will be home in a couple of hours and we can have a late dinner."

Hope smiled as he picked up the Epsom salts and bath beads she had put in. He looked like he wanted to pour them in but based on his frown he couldn't figure out how much to pour. "Here let me take care of that while you get out of your wet clothes."

Warrick smiled and kissed her gently before nodding, "Deal, I'll be home in three hours max. I expect you to be thoroughly relaxed by then."

WARRICK PEELED himself out of the wet clothes and dried off as he watched Hope prepare her bath. She was beautiful on the outside but it was her inner beauty that drew him to her. Her ready smile and the way she easily helped out others. He thought she looked like a small ray of sunshine as a little girl. Not even his imagination of what she would have grown up to be like could have done her justice.

Warrick used the towel to dry off, and hanging his clothes over the wall of the shower, for a moment, he reluctantly tore his eyes from her body to walk out of the bathroom to get dressed. All the men on patrol worked in pairs and he knew that the one he was paired up would be showing up any minute.

Dressed in clean clothes and dry boots he walked into the bathroom and kissed her one last time, right before she stepped into the tub. "I'll be back soon."

Hope gave him an inviting smile before he walked away, causing his cock to swell and press against his zipper. Warrick grabbed his jacket on the way out of his room to head downstairs and await his partner.

He understood why he wasn't normally patrolling. They didn't want to leave either him or Hope alone and give his brother an opening to try and take either of them. The only reason they let him go for a few hours today was because Damien was still next-door and was going to be keeping an eye on the house. With his twin connection to her he didn't have to be watching her to know if something was wrong.

Once downstairs he heard a knock on the door. Opening it he saw Max, one of the newest wolf guards. He was the youngest in his family and the only boy. His father had passed away a few years ago and he was trying his best to support his mother and three sisters. He was eager to learn and had excelled at hand-to-hand combat. Despite all his hardships, Max always showed up with a smile on his face and was often the first to show up for training and the last to leave. He had quickly become one of Chase's favorite trainees and Warrick couldn't help but smile at the young wolf whose hazel green eyes looked to be dancing with mischief as he stood on his porch.

"Am I early?" Max asked as Warrick stepped out onto the porch.

"No, you're on time. I just had to change my clothes after working with Damien all day." Warrick replied as he locked the front door to the house.

Max nodded and Warrick noticed how he shot a glance at his still wet hair. Warrick smiled to himself as they headed out. The memory of Hope lying naked in the tub, her smile and the way she felt, squirming in his arms as he tickled her, was a hell of a memory for him to take on patrol. She was everything he had dreamt of over the years, and so much more.

He looked up to see Damien in the upstairs window. With a nod in his direction, he and Max started walking towards the outskirts of the town. Aithne had mapped out different patrol areas and with the help of Chase, the two of them were able to come up with a plan that covered the most area with the least amount of people.

"Do you really think your brother will be stupid enough to come back and try something?" Max asked.

"I do," Warrick said sighing as he looked around. "I'd hoped he wouldn't, but once he showed up…"

Max nodded and both of them continued patrolling in silence. Warrick couldn't help feeling like he was being watched. The hair on the back of his neck stuck up. His wolf inside him began to pace and he could hear his soft growl. Looking over at Max he asked, "Have you seen or noticed anything?"

Max looked around and shook his head. "No, am I missing something?"

Warrick shook his head. Max's words made him think he might be imagining it. It was over an hour before he would be relieved of duty, yet that odd feeling of being watched never left him. When his relief showed up neither he nor Jeremy acted like anything was wrong, making him doubt himself even more.

18

Hope knew something was wrong when Warrick came home from his patrol. When she asked if something had happened he shrugged and said nothing. With his silence, she knew something had changed. Warrick was guarded and they didn't make love that night. Instead he held her, kissing her gently while cupping her cheek and telling her to rest for their sparring session tomorrow night.

Sandra showed up after Warrick left, bringing Hope coffee and a donut. "Hey stranger, I thought I would check in on you," Sandra said, giving her a small hug while standing in the door with her goodies.

Hope smiled, grabbing the drink tray. "If it makes you feel better I've been getting abused and beat up every day I've been away." Sandra gave her a look and Hope shrugged. "Apparently, besides being my brothers mate, Kassandra enjoys kicking my ass and calling it training."

Sandra laughed as she took a donut from the back before tossing it to her. "Well she is one of the dragon guards."

With a shrug and a small guilty smile Hope replied, "True, but she's also family, so I thought she was going to take it easier on me." Sandra gave her a look and they both laughed. Kassandra would push her harder as her sister. If anything ever happened to Hope, Kassandra would blame herself for not training her better.

"Okay so I know you are busy tonight but how about girl's night tomorrow?" Sandra asked. "You could probably use a break. We can do it at my place. I was thinking all the women who helped us finish up the houses. As a reward."

Hope nodded, "That would be a great idea. I might have to have Warrick or Damien drop me off and pick me up since I promised not to go anywhere alone…"

"Why don't I pick you up instead? We can go shopping today if that's okay and tomorrow night we can pick up whatever we forgot, because there is always something, and Warrick can pick you up in the morning. That way we can drink…a lot."

"That could be doable. I am not sure he will agree to let me stay the night though."

Sandra looked at her neck and raised an eyebrow. "I see that you two finally, umm…"

Hope blushed nodding. It was interesting having everyone know that he had claimed her and that they had made love. Your private life wasn't always so private as a wolf. She wore her mark proudly. Not once thinking of covering it up but she found herself blushing when she noticed other's looking. The men, she noticed, sometimes would pat Warrick on the back while the women smiled and nodded in her direction.

"By that blush on your cheeks I am going to guess more than once. And that you enjoyed yourself." Hope felt herself blushing more, which made Sandra laugh harder. "Good for you. It's about time your mate claimed you."

Hope took a sip of her coffee. She didn't want to go into details with Sandra about her and Warrick in bed. She did notice the change in the women's attitude toward him after they noticed her mark but she didn't feel the need to go into details. That was private, between her and Warrick, and she wanted it to stay that way.

Sandra gave her a grin before letting that conversation drop. "So what are you doing today? Any plans?"

Hope shook her head, "No. Today I'm just staying in. Thought I'd give my shadows the day off."

"That's nice of you. Have they gotten any closer to catching Gabriel? I can't believe he made it all the way into town without anyone seeing him."

"No. As of right now we aren't even sure if he's still close by or if he left," Hope said with a sigh. "It's like he knew Warrick was starting to be happy and came in to ruin it."

Hope heard the pout in her own voice before she took a bite of her food. Sandra reached over and patted her on the hand, making her smile. It was nice having female friends. Her brother, Damien, was nice, but sympathetic he was not. He just told her to have faith that he would kick any ass that needed to be kicked. It did make her smile but she wanted to take a minute to wallow in self-pity. She didn't want to live there, just throw a small pity party where she got to stomp her feet and throw a tantrum before moving on. Damien always gave her this look, like she was crazy, when she said that. Maybe it was a girl thing.

Sandra smiled, taking the last bite of her donut. "Okay I'm off. Text me tomorrow and let me know when I can pick you up. We can get drinks on the way to my house and I'll have the girls help bring in the junk food."

Hope walked her to the door giving her a hug. She watched her walk out to her car waving before smiling to the guard who was patrolling the house. With Warrick gone for the day she knew Damien had made sure there would be at least two on the house. Kassandra even had one that tailed her when she was on her own, which made Hope feel only slightly better.

Making another pot of coffee to share with the guards outside, she smiled thinking about being able to spar with Warrick tonight. Her wolf had been itching to come out since they've mated and she was looking forward to it, probably more than she should. Pouring each a cup she headed outside to find them.

WARRICK LOOKED outside the window as he and Damien drove out of town. Aithne had been able to track down a rumor about the witch's coven. His mind wandered to his dreams of last night. Gabriel was there, and tied to the table was Hope. She was covered in so much blood and her body was still as his brother stood over her. He wanted to move but his body was frozen.

"I can see why you couldn't resist her, brother. She is beautiful." Gabriel looked down at her body licking his lips causing Warrick's stomach to roll. "So passionate."

Warrick closed his eyes and another wave of nausea hit him. He could feel his wolf itching to come out. "She cried out for you at first. But after the third time I took her she forgot you ever existed." Making a tsking noise Gabriel looked at him, "So selfish brother. You're supposed to keep her safe. Instead you're the reason I had to kill her."

He was suddenly able to move and Warrick attacked him them. Blinded by rage he went for his brother's throat. Before he could wrap his hands around him, he felt the cold steel slide deep into his belly. As he fell to the ground he looked up and saw his brother, Gabriel, smiling down at him. "Soon my brother, you will get to watch her die before I kill you for real."

When he finally woke up that morning he'd held Hope tight. She whimpered a bit before curling up closer to him, laying on his chest. She had nuzzled him as if sensing his need to hold her. Warrick never wanted to let her go. When the sun came up in the morning he watched as the light shone on her hair. The different shades of blonde and gold glittered in the light.

He watched as she yawned and stretched, her eyes slowly coming open, a light blush on her cheeks as she looked up at him. Her amber eyes still held a bit of sleep and he stroked her hair. There was a moment, when she looked at him, that he forgot about the dream, forgot about the world around them, and it was just the two of them.

She was his world and if he had to kill his twin brother to keep her safe...he wouldn't even hesitate.

"I would ask you what you are thinking about but based on the growls I hear coming from you I would bet it has something to do with your brother," Damien said interrupting his thoughts.

With a shake of his head Warrick tore his gaze from the window to look at Damien. "I think my brother is trying to mess with me."

He was surprised when he heard Damien give a laugh. He looked over at his mate's brother thinking he might have lost his mind when Damien finally spoke up. "Your brother has been torturing you most of your life. Stole everything he could. Your brother, for a lack of a better word, is a rabid dog that needs to be put down."

Warrick felt a moment of guilt. Gabriel was his brother. If he never imprinted on Hope they never would have had their life turned upside down. "You can blame yourself for your brother all you want to. You are no more responsible for his actions than Hope is for mine."

"He told me once that if I escaped and mated with Hope he would kill her. I should have stayed away," Warrick said not even trying to hide his disgust with himself.

Damien was silent for so long that Warrick finally turned and looked at him. "Are you done feeling sorry for yourself?" Damien finally asked him. "Staying away would have only hurt my sister more. Her whole life she missed you. Cried over you. This situation isn't ideal but your brother is responsible for his own actions. Your only job is to love my sister and protect her. I know you've been trying to do that second one on your own but now it's time to ask for help and rely on the rest of us while you work on that first one. Hope's waited long enough for you and now it's time you make her happy and love her like she deserves."

Warrick nodded. It was hard not to take the blame for his brother but Damien was right and his job as Hope's mate was clear. There was something humbling about hearing how Hope might have cried for him. He would keep her safe and spend the rest of his life making up for any tears she might have shed for him...but first he needed to find his brother.

19

Hope was giddy with excitement while they ate dinner that night. Not wanting anything heavy she'd made them a salad with baked chicken that she used lemons and herbs to season. They were going to train in their back yard since it was a big, wide open area and the guards were told to stay close enough to hear the alpha's howl for help but not so close as to disturb them.

Warrick had told her they would start about an hour after dinner giving her time to digest her food while he walked the perimeter. When he pulled her close and gave her a quick, hard kiss she almost melted into him. When he pulled away he told her to meet him outside in an hour. Hope bobbed her head in agreement. Since no one was going to be around so she didn't need to dress to go outside. She hated tearing her clothes when she shifted. Hope had a little bit of magic envy of how the dragons were able to shred their clothes with magic when they shifted and have those pieces rematerialize when they shifted back to their human form.

She had asked Kassandra about it the first time she saw her do it. Kassandra laughed and replied, "I turn into a beast that the god's created to destroy things. I guess when they turned us human they left some magic with us and our ancestors had asked for that ability."

Hope shook her head. It was amazing the things that one took for granted. Humans never knew of shifters but she imagined if they did they would want to understand how their body changed. How it was that after a year or so shifting, the pain they first felt, went away. They were aware of the fact that their bones were breaking and re-lengthening, muscles changing but it no longer hurt. That first shift as a teenager was painful but each one after was less and less until it no longer hurt.

Hope looked at the clock and went to stand on the porch. The sun was just starting to set. Sniffing the air, she could smell Warrick. He was close but not quite visible yet. She was also aware of the guards. Her wolf, itching to come out, was close to the surface and told her that they were not close enough to see her. As she kicked off her shoes she started to pull off her shirt. Folding it she put it on the chair on the back porch. When she removed the rest of her clothes she folded everything nicely.

As she stood up she became aware of Warrick coming up the back yard. He was naked already and the light from the fading sun shone off his body. Her eyes greedily took him in. When they'd found him months ago he was skin and bones and barely alive, now before her was a strong healthy man. Each day he got stronger and most days she could barely detect his limp. She traced the muscles from his strong thighs up his body. He didn't have a six-pack but she could see his muscle definition and that line that ran along his hips made her mouth water. When she noticed his cock starting to harden as he stood there, she finally raised her eyes up to his.

He smirked as if he could read her mind and she realized that with their connection and enhanced since of smell he probably could. She walked down the stairs slowly keeping her eyes locked on his. Testing their connection, she spoke to him through their link *Are you ready?*

Hope felt his eyes caressing her body before she heard him respond. *I've been waiting for you.*

His voice felt like a caress and a shiver ran up her spine at his words. There was just a hint of promise. When they were about five feet from each other they stopped. Warrick had a look on his face that made her pause.

"If I hurt you..." Warrick started to say when Hope let out a small laugh.

"You won't," she whispered giving him a grin. She knew without a doubt that he would never hurt her.

His eyes lit up and he nodded. There was a moment when they both stood staring at each other. Her wolf knew what was coming up and as if on silent cue, they began to circle each other taking steps back. He was handsome. His scars added a mystery to him. He was hers, destined by the Fates, and now that she had a taste of him she would spend the rest of her life fighting to keep him.

When they were far enough apart he gave her a nod and they both shifted. Her bones breaking and reshaping, being put together by magic as her body changed into the wolf. When the transformations were complete she stood, proud, before him. Her wolf taking in his, they circled each other.

She had never seen him in his wolf form before. Warrick was dark in color, not as dark as her brother was, but his fur was a dark brown with a white patch of fur that ran under his chest. His eyes changed colors from cobalt blue to hazel with hints of yellow peeking through. Alpha's tended to stand a little taller and she guessed his wolf stood about as tall as her brother.

In this form she was even more aware of their connection. She could feel his desire for her and the need to protect her. There were other feelings as well but those two were the strongest. His need to protect her made her want to show him how strong she really was. He needed to know she could protect herself and that when it came down to it she could help guard his back.

Warrick lunged at her and she growled baring her teeth. She knew he could jump higher than her so she paused for a split second before lunging at him. Her goal was to come up underneath him. When she got close to his throat with her teeth she felt him use his front legs to push hard into her side.

Knocking the wind out of her as she fell back on her side. She felt his concern and got up shaking her head, letting him know she wanted to continue. Her teeth bared she looked for an opening when he charged her again. This time the two of them hit chest to chest. The force of the hit rattled her. Warrick was probably a hundred pounds heavier than her in this form and maybe a foot taller.

That put her in a position where leverage was her friend. She was lower on his chest and with the lower center of gravity she was able to hold him off. The only unfortunate part was that with his weight, she doubted she could outlast him. Doing something she learned as a child, she let her weight slip on one side causing him to slide against her as she nipped at his hind leg before jumping away.

She heard his chuckle and a growly voice in her head *Good job*. She almost smiled and the two of them attacked each other again. As they continued to spar in wolf form, Hope began to feel more confident.

He pinned her once from behind him and she bumped him again as he held her neck down. His teeth did not break the skin, instead he just held her still while she wiggled her body under his. The movement was completely erotic and when he let out a warming growl she grinned to herself and wiggled again.

Hope could smell the subtle shift in the air and new he was feeling it too. When he finally released her Hope rolled back to her feet and stood up on all fours. Ready for a change she shifted back to her human form. Her body was covered in a light sweat and she grinned at the wolf that watched her wearily.

A grin playing on her lips. "Catch me if you can."

With that she ran. She knew that everyone was told to give them room in the back to spar so she didn't worry about running into anyone. She felt him behind her running quickly. His wolf nipped at her leg and she laughed. She knew he was close and he was just letting her run.

Hope gave in to the urge to look behind her. He was so close, she squealed in excitement. When she felt something hit her toe she cried out as she fell forward. Before she hit the ground she felt an arm wrap around her and pull her close. Warrick had shifted faster than anyone she had ever seen before and managed to catch her before she fell.

"Are you okay?" he asked. Hope nodded, shuddering as she felt his warm breath against her ear.

"How did you..." she started to ask as she looked over her shoulder at him. Her breath caught at the hungry look in his eyes.

Warrick nuzzled the side of her neck making her moan as she tilted her head to give him better access, "After that first shift I was able to shift quickly. My dad said my grandfather had the same ability."

Hope nodded, her eyes closing as she let out a small sigh. When Warrick nipped at the base of her neck her legs shook under her. When she pressed back against him she heard his growl as her backside brushed against his cock.

In one swift move he bent and picked her up. Hope wrapped her arms around his neck, nuzzling him as he took quick strides to the house. A small giggle escaping her as she kissed along his neck. "I can walk."

He grunted before looking down at her. "We shouldn't risk it."

She nodded, biting her lip. The look on his face telling her he had no intention of letting her go. He wanted her. That knowledge sent a shiver up her spine and she smiled as she sucked on his earlobe, making love to it like a small cock. She felt him adjust his hold as he opened the door. She didn't pay attention as they went up the stairs; instead she kissed and licked every part she could reach.

20

Warrick felt his cock kick every time Hope's teeth scraped along his sensitive flesh. He didn't think he was going to make it up the stairs. He thought about taking her right there but with his wolf so close to the surface he didn't think he could be gentle and he didn't want to bruise her soft skin.

Back when she shifted into her human form and told him to chase her she called out to every animal instinct to chase and capture his mate. When she had almost tripped he quickly shifted and managed to grab her before she fell, causing her naked body to press against his. If there weren't guards nearby he might have given in to his need and taken her out there. But he knew if one came to close, the wolf's need to protect its mate would surface and he would attack him.

When he finally walked in the room he gently placed her in the middle of the bed. Her arm's wrapped around his neck he followed her down. Warrick felt Hope kiss along his jaw until she got to his to mouth. Claiming her lips with his, he kissed her deeply, sliding his tongue against hers as their bodies writhed together.

His hands sliding up to touch her breasts, cupping them, gently squeezing, loving the way her body arched under him. Hope broke the kiss as her head tilted back, pushing her breasts deeper into his hands. When she sighed his name, "Warrick," he bent his head and took one of her lovely pink tipped nipples into his mouth.

Every whimper, every moan from her lips stroked his male ego. Her fingers slid into his hair, pulling as he held her to his breast. When he released the first breast to go to the next he heard her whimper in protest, her nails digging into his scalp. When he turned his head to make love to the next one, he heard her soft cry of pleasure, "Oh Gods yes, Warrick."

He nipped at the hard nub first before kissing away the small sting. Her hips writhing under him, her body already wet and ready. He slipped his cock between her folds as her hips continued to roll beneath his.

Warrick released her breast to kiss and lick along her belly. When he got to her belly button he nipped at her gently, loving the way her muscles quivered under his touch. Before he settled between her thighs he grinned and used his hands to flip her over.

"Warrick," Hope said with a small laugh. He gave in to temptation and smacked her ass playfully before kneeling between her legs. Placing his hands on her hips, he gripped them tight before pulling her to her knees in one swift motion.

His wolf almost howled in delight at the view before him. Her head down, her back arched up presenting her beautiful ass for his view. This submissive position was what his wolf needed. He reached down teasing her with his fingers and finding her clit easily. The nub hard and eager for his attention. As he strummed it, he felt her hips push back against him and she let out a small whimper.

When he felt like she was close, he positioned his cock at her entrance and pushed in slowly. Hope's warm heat surrounded him. When he was deep inside her, he let out a moan holding still for a moment to appreciate how good she felt surrounding him.

Hope moved under him encouraging him to move and he smiled as he looked down at her. Holding her hips still with his hands he pulled out almost completely before slamming back in deep. Her answering cries of pleasure encouraged him to do it again. Every time she cried out in pleasure he felt his need for her grow.

When he could no longer hold back he slid one hand under her and started playing with her clit. She gasped softly as her hips began to buck on their own against him. As the walls of her core started rippling around him he knew she was as close as he was.

When he felt her go over, heard her scream, Warrick was no longer able to hold back. Both of his hands gripped her hips as he pulled her closer to him letting her muscles quiver as he went over the edge with her. Each time her muscles quivered around him he felt another wave of pleasure.

When they both came down, his cock softened and slipped from her core. With a sigh he watched as she fell forward. Leaning forward he bit and kissed her shoulder before rolling to her side. Her blonde hair covered her face and he reached up a hand and brushed it back to look at her. He saw the hint of a smile playing on her lips before she turned to cuddle up with him.

"Would love to know what you were thinking about that had you smiling so?" Warrick asked as he stroked her hair.

Hope giggled before she looked up at him. Her amber eyes dancing with mischief and she smiled bigger. "I was thinking that training with you has way more perks than training with Kassandra."

Warrick laughed gently, swatting her ass, "Let's just keep it that way."

Her laughter filled the room and he pulled her into his arms. He loved the way her face softened when she was happy. Warrick kissed the top of her head as she settled against his chest. She had one leg thrown over his and her head rested on his chest.

Warrick felt his body relax under her. Hope was a light in the dark. As he continued to idly stroke her back he felt her fall asleep. He was baffled by the way she openly trusted him. He had been the source of so much pain in her life and yet she didn't seem to blame him for anything.

A yawn escaped him and he snuggled closer to her as he felt

himself drift off. His dreams filled with images of blonde hair, a willing body and laughter.

Warrick stretched as he woke up but reaching out to find her he frowned when he realized he was in bed alone. He looked around and rubbed his face. The faintest smell of coffee hit him and he smiled. As much as he liked waking up to coffee in the morning he preferred waking up to her in his arms.

He got up and took care of his personal needs, putting on a pair of sweat pants before heading downstairs. When he walked into the kitchen he grinned seeing her bent over as she rummaged through the fridge. She was wearing his shirt and those adorable boy-short underwear. He loved the way the underside of her peeked out begging for his attention. He reached out and caressed her ass, chuckling when she jumped.

"I was going to make you breakfast in bed," she said with a small pout, her lower lip sticking out prettily.

Warrick didn't even fight the temptation but instead leaned in and kissed her gently. "Why don't I help you cook and we can both enjoy breakfast in bed."

He felt her lips curve in a smile as she nodded. "Eggs and bacon sound okay?" She asked causing him to look down to see what she had in her hands.

"Perfect. I'll take care of the bacon and you can make the eggs." He took them from her. Noticing that she had already heated up a pan, he opened the package and started cooking. Warrick smiled when Hope made him a cup of coffee and brought it to him.

"Thank you," he said pulling her close before she could step away. "As nice as breakfast in bed is I prefer to wake up with you."

He watched as a soft blush spread on Hope's cheeks. She was so sweet and easily embarrassed. She was utterly adorable. "I'll remember that next time."

When he was close to finishing the bacon she started the eggs.

They made up their plates and refilled their cups both heading upstairs. They settled into the bed, their bodies touching. They ate in a comfortable silence.

When they'd finished eating they sipped their coffee in silence. He felt her shift and take his hand, lacing her fingers with his. Warrick looked down at their joined hands. Hope's was so much smaller than his; her fingers were long, thin and soft. He brought her hand up to his lips and kissed it.

"What are you doing today?" Warrick asked curiously.

"Kassandra thought we should stat painting the daycare. There were a few single moms who wanted to go back to work and so we wanted to open a preschool for them. And then tonight is girl's night with Sandra."

Warrick nodded frowning. "Just make sure you don't go anywhere tonight alone. I know she's taking you there but do you mind if I pick you up."

Hope gave him a smile and she nodded, "I promise to be safe tonight and would love it if you picked me up."

21

Hope smiled when Sandra showed up. After painting and cleaning all day with Kassandra she was eager to do something fun. It seemed like all they had been doing for the past few weeks had been training and working. Girl's night was a much-needed distraction.

"Hey are you ready to go?" Sandra asked as she gave her a kiss on the cheek.

"Beyond ready," Hope said with a smile. "It's been way too long since I've gone out with just the girls."

Sandra smiled as they got into the car. Her place was a small house on the opposite side of town. Hope listened to Sandra talk as they drove. She chatted about the food she had bought and how she was looking forward to having drinks with her. "I forgot to ask. Are you staying the night or is Warrick picking you up?"

"Warrick's going to come and get me," Hope said blushing just thinking about the night before and the nice quiet morning they'd spent together. When he admitted he would rather wake up with her than have her make breakfast in bed she found herself loving him a little more.

She loved him. Not because she was bound to him but because of who he was. Despite everything he had been through, he was still a good person. He was always careful with her and when she watched him with the younger witch sisters he was patient.

Sandra laughed. "I am going to take that color in your cheeks and faraway look in your eyes to mean the two of you are doing well."

Hope nodded, smiling. "We are."

When they pulled up to Sandra's house, Hope frowned while looking around. She had expected to see cars in the driveway and was surprised to see no one else there. "I thought the other girls were meeting us here?"

"They are. They should be here in a little bit," Sandra told her as she got out of her car.

Hope had a feeling that something was off. Her hand on the door she hesitated before shrugging it off. Everyone had been on edge since seeing Gabriel and she was just feeling paranoid. After all, Sandra had been nothing but nice to her.

After convincing herself she was acting crazy, Hope followed Sandra to the front door. The sun had just set and Hope noticed that most of the houses next to Sandra's were still empty. In the next few days some of the smaller families were scheduled to move in but for now all the dark homes seemed to be fueling her paranoia.

The door opened and Sandra smiled over her shoulder. "Okay let's heat up some of the food I bought before the girls get here."

Without turning on any lights they walked to the back of the house where the kitchen was. As they stepped into the kitchen the light came on and Hope almost `fell back against the wall.

Gabriel was sitting at the table.

Before she could turn and run she felt Sandra reach out and grab her. Stronger than she looked, Hope struggled against her as Gabriel stood up making a tsking sound of displeasure, "Hope, it's so good to finally meet you."

Hope felt her skin crawl as he reached out and touched her cheek. She struggled against Sandra when she realized that even this close she could not smell Gabriel. There was the faintest smell of sulfur when he stood close to her, but that was it.

She knew that she couldn't take them both on so she relaxed, deciding to save her energy and keep her wits about her so she could figure out a way to escape. She hadn't yet told Warrick she loved him and he deserved to know that.

"I would have met you years ago Gabriel, had you not killed my father... or yours," Hope said, giving him her best look of indifference.

Gabriel chuckled stepping back, "Very true. I guess I should've tried to kill you myself and not left it to those dogs. Who would've thought two young pups could've outsmarted them."

Sandra turned her around and Hope felt Gabriel grab her arms, tying them together with rope. Her skin crawled having him this close. Her wolf, howling, wanted to shift. Stronger in her wolf form she started to feel her skin begin to itch. Before she could give in to the urge she felt a collar go around her neck. Once it was secure it felt like a barrier was up disconnecting her from her wolf. The feeling of being suddenly alone terrified her and then she heard him whisper. "Just something to keep your beast in check."

Hope struggled against the binds and when he was directly behind her she swung her head back effectively head butting him in the face. He made a low growl sound then stepped back from her. Before she could enjoy her small moment of triumph she felt a hand smack her against the face, hard enough to leave a stinging impression on her cheek.

"Bitch," Sandra gritted, a look of pure hatred on her face.

Hope was more surprised by the look on the girl's face than the smack she'd just received. "Why are you doing this Sandra?"

Sandra's upper lip pulled back in a snarl and as she repeated the question, her voice sounding unusually high. "Why, why am I doing this? Maybe, because thanks to you I lost everything. I was to be his mate once you and Warrick were gone. We had it all planned out, we just needed to find your mother first and those witches would've sealed our place at the head of both packs."

"What do you mean find my mother?" Hope asked. "I thought you..." her voice trailed off. If Gabriel didn't know where her mother was, did that mean that her mother had escaped? How come they hadn't heard anything?

Gabriel laughed as he grabbed a towel, putting a part of it into her mouth before wrapping it around the back of her head and tying it in place. "I'm looking forward to seeing Warrick's face when he finds out that I have you."

Hope knew that Warrick's guilt would kill him. She felt her heart twist in pain for her mate. Gabriel gave her a wicked grin before she felt something heavy strike the back of her head causing her world to go black.

22

Warrick felt a stab of pain in the back of his head but shook it off when he faintly heard Hope's voice. He had been feeling anxious all day today. When he came home he was happy to see Jared standing there letting him know that he saw Hope leave a few minutes ago with her friend and that the dragons were relieving the wolves for the night.

Jared was one of the dragons that had helped save him and they had become fast friends. Jared could have chosen to be a very rich playboy; instead he dedicated himself to helping his people and those that needed help. From the little he'd learned about Jared, his family did not approve of his choice to be a member of the king's guard, even went as far as to threaten to cut him off. Jared never mentioned his family but he knew it was a sore subject.

Warrick walked outside feeling anxious. It was early and he didn't expect to hear from Hope so soon but he couldn't shake the feeling that something was wrong. "If I didn't know any better I'd say you were missing your mate," Jared said as he walked up the trail to the porch.

With a shrug, Warrick rubbed the back of his neck, which made

Jared laugh. "I just can't shake this feeling..." Warrick started to say, feeling like he sounded a bit paranoid.

Jared opened his mouth to respond when they both heard the sound of a motorcycle pulling up...fast. He recognized it immediately as Damien's. At the speed he was going Warrick found himself worried he wouldn't be able to stop in time.

Damien came to a screeching halt in front of them. He took his helmet off quickly giving him a look that worried Warrick. "Where's Hope?"

Before he could answer, Damien was in front of him grabbing his shirt, the paniced look on his face the only thing keeping Warrick from pushing him off him. "Where is she? I can't feel her."

"She went to Sandra's for girl's night." Warrick said, a feeling of panic starting to set in. "What do you mean you can't feel her?"

Damien realized he was still holding onto Warrick and released him. "I felt a moment of panic and sadness and then nothing...it was like she just disappeared."

Warrick felt himself starting to lose control, his wolf coming near the surface trying to find it's mate through their link. Since newly mated, their connection wasn't that strong but he couldn't feel her either.

Before Warrick could start to go into an all-out panic he felt Jared touch his arm. "Before you do anything rash, let's head over there and see what's going on."

Warrick nodded, glad when Jared pointed out that his truck was parked close by and offering to drive. They sped through the town and Warrick had the door open and was out of the truck before it even came to a complete stop.

He was up on the front porch, Damien at his heels before Jared had finished putting his vehicle into park. No lights on in the house, Warrick banged on the door before turning the handle. It was unlocked and without even stopping to think about it Warrick charged in.

Damien growled as they both walked in following her scent to the kitchen. Hope's smell stopped there in the doorway. He could smell

Sandra but that was it. It was like the two of them just disappeared without a trace.

Jared came in through the back door. "I can see the smallest hint of a trail outside but I can't detect a scent from anyone."

"We need to follow it." Warrick started to go, when Damien grabbed him by the arm. Warrick bared his teeth, turning around with a snarl. "Let me go."

Damien snapped back, lengthening his teeth. "She's my sister but if I let you go after her and something happens, she'll kill me."

Jared blocked the door while holding the phone to his ear. He distantly heard him talking to someone. The ringing in his ears was muffled by the sound of his wolf howling. He wanted to run after her but Damien was right, what good would it do to charge after her. Gabriel managed to kidnap her without leaving much of a trace. If Gabriel managed to hide her scent and conceal her from her mate connection as well as her twin connection, then that trail was mostly left for them to find on purpose.

"Viktor and Chase are on their way. Aithne is coordinating rescue parties to start searching the woods." Jared paused looking at Warrick, his face softening. "You have to trust Hope to keep herself alive. We'll find her."

Warrick nodded, knowing he wasn't the only one who was fighting the urge to charge head long to find her. The sound of a car pulling up got their attention. The door flew open and Kassandra ran into the living room. Her eyes going instantly to Damien.

"I got here as soon as I could," she said walking to him. "We'll find her." She looked at Warrick and frowned. "What do you know about Sandra?"

"Not a lot. She befriended Hope when they started working on the finishing touches on the houses so families could move in. She only stopped by for a minute. Have you met her?"

Kassandra frowned thinking about it. "No. Whenever she was supposed to go places with the two of us, she cancelled. What does she look like?"

Warrick frowned, "Pretty average. Little shorter than Hope, dark hair, brown eyes average build."

He watched as Kassandra thought about it. "The only girl I really remember was the one that was on Gabriel's lap when we got there. I wonder if…"

Damien nodded. "There were other women helping out. I think there's a list in the office. Maybe they'll know if she's the same one."

Kassandra nodded, cupping Damien's cheek before she walked over to Warrick and gave him a hug. Surprised, he stood stiffly until she pulled back. "I promise we'll find her."

With that, she left as quickly as she had appeared. Warrick ran his fingers through his hair, frustrated. What was he expected to do? Just sit and wait? He knew what kind of torture his brother was able to come up with. He had practiced on him and perfected it over the years. If Gabriel was hurting her he would kill him.

With a growl of frustration Warrick punched the wall. He felt his bones hitting the plaster and the pain at what he had done but none of it made him feel better. He needed Hope. This feeling was worse than enduring the torture he'd suffered at Gabriel's hands. From the moment Hope put her hands on his cheek and called him hers, Warrick would do anything to protect her.

Chase and Viktor both showed up a few minutes later. Warrick had been fighting the urge to shift and when they both showed up looking calmer than him, he fought the urge to punch them both in the face.

"Your brother's not going to hurt her," Chase said as if he knew for sure. "He just wants to get in your head. This is all about you. Can you think of any place that means something to the both of you?"

"The only place I could possibly think would be our childhood home. But I don't think that's standing anymore," Warrick said, pacing again while tuning them out. He was thinking about every horrible thing his brother could be doing right now.

After a few minutes, Jared touched his arm. "Warrick, let's go home. If Gabriel reaches out to you, I think it will be there."

Looking around he saw that Viktor, Chase and Damien were all watching him. Warrick had a feeling they might have been talking to him before Jared got his attention. "I can't go home. What if…"

Damien shook his head. "She's my sister and I want her found as badly as you do. But I agree, this is a head game for your brother. Whatever game he's trying to play involves you." Damien paused, waiting for him to nod. "Kassandra can go invisible and mask her scent completely. She's going to go home with you. I don't want you alone. He's not getting his hands on both of you."

"He's going to want me alone. If it comes down to her or me—"

"I'll sacrifice you in a heartbeat," Damien said his amber eyes never leaving Warrick's. "But they'll never know Kassandra's with you and she *will* be with you. I will track her through our connection. Hope will kill me if I let anything happen to you. Your brother does *not* get to win."

A look at Chase and Viktor told him they all agreed with the plan. It was true. Gabriel was after him and in the end Warrick knew that Gabriel could never take his place as pack alpha. When Damien and Hope showed up, all of Gabriel's plans had been ruined.

"Where's Kassandra?" Warrick asked.

23

Hope moaned as she tried to open her eyes. Her left eye was swollen. Whatever was suppressing her wolf had also managed to suppress her healing ability. She had a funny feeling she had a black eye but there was no mirror. The rag was still stuffed in her mouth and she tried to move her jaw from side to side. It was tender but hurt less than her eye, which she guessed would soon be swollen shut if movies were to be believed.

As she looked around she realized they had dumped her into a room alone. There was some light coming in from the window and she could see a bed and a dresser but not much else. From the smell, she would guess they were in a room that had not been used in a long time. The room itself smelled stale, as if neither the door nor the windows had been opened in a long time.

Trying to stand was difficult with her hands tied behind her back but after some maneuvering she was able to get up on her feet. As a twin, Hope had always felt Damien through their connection, but with it cut off, for the first time, she felt totally alone. But if she couldn't feel him, then he couldn't feel her and whatever time they had hoped to gain would be cut short. Telepathic connection between twins wasn't uncommon among shifters but she doubted anyone had known how strong the two of theirs actually was.

Damien would have gone right by Warrick to find her and Warrick would have known what happened. It wouldn't have taken them long to figure everything out. Her chest hurt at the thought of Warrick feeling guilty about this, or that her brother Damien might blame him.

Walking toward the window Hope looked outside. Woods surrounded the house they were in. There were no other houses or roads in sight. She wondered if the two of them had taken her to one of the many cabins that ran along the woods in the mountains. There were hundreds of acres of land and many cabins, not to mention that the area they lived in had more than one mountain close by.

Hope found herself wishing she at least had her wolf's night vision as she looked around the room. She needed something to help untie the binds on her wrist. The room was pretty sparse, a small twin bed, a dresser and a chair. Based on the stale air she was willing to bet everything was covered in a layer of dust. The closest thing to a sharp edge was a rounded corner on the windowsill.

With a sigh Hope turned around and began to use the edge of the windowsill as she tried her best to pull the ropes open. As she rubbed the rope on the rounded edge she realized what she was doing was mostly futile. Without being able to shift enough to make her claws grow she felt useless. She should have had Kassandra teach her how to escape. Maybe she would have been better at that than defending herself from Gabriel.

The house was pretty quiet but Hope didn't think that meant she was alone in the house. She listened intently as she rubbed the rope up and down on the windowsill. Her thoughts naturally drifted to Warrick and Damien. She hoped her brother wasn't too hard on Warrick, he would already blame himself and didn't need her brother in his head.

She hoped Warrick knew that his brother was using her as bait and that he wouldn't fall for it. There was no doubt in her mind that Warrick would come for her, she just hoped it wasn't to sacrifice himself. Hope needed him to fight for her, for himself, for the future they deserved together. She needed him to know that she loved him. Not just because they were mated but also because despite everything he was still the most selfless person she knew. He always put her and his people first. With everything he had been through, he was still kind and gentle.

A sound outside her door made her pause. One of the floorboards creaked and she saw a shadow of someone standing in front of the door. As the door slowly opened, she took a step away from the window and used her nails to scratch at the pieces of rope she could feel had been rubbing on the curve. When the light revealed Sandra instead of Gabriel she narrowed her eyes.

"What are you doing here?" She asked as she watched her walk in. "Where's Gabriel?"

Sandra smirked as she pulled out a knife and began to play with it. "Gabriel went to go and find your mate and bring him here."

Hope felt her heart tighten in fear for him. She watched as Sandra continued to move the knife so that it caught the light coming in from the window. "Why are you doing this Sandra? Why are you helping Gabriel? He doesn't care about anyone––"

"He loves me," Sandra shouted at her as she took a step deeper into the room. "He wanted to claim me since I was young. Told me how his brother had stolen everything from him. That we just had to wait until the witches could find a way that we no longer needed yours and Warrick's connection so I could rule by his side."

Hope laughed shaking her head. "What did Warrick steal? He was first born and the rightful alpha, he was my mate...determined by the Fates. What claim did Gabriel have to anything? He was a second son and if he really was your mate he would have given everything up to be with you. Don't you know how mating works?"

The look Sandra gave her was one of pure hate. "That's not true. You know nothing."

Hope smiled as she felt the rope move slightly. She was able to use her fingers to work the knot as best she could. "Are you sure? Because my mate was willing to sacrifice himself for years to make sure I was safe and happy. Endured torture at Gabriel's hand just to keep me safe. Someone he met a few times as a young kid. Gabriel wouldn't give up anything for you--"

Before she could finish Sandra yelled and charged at her. The knife held in the air as if she planned to stab her with it. Hope waited for the last minute until she moved low and used her body to hit Sandra, knocking her into the wall, causing her to drop the knife. With her hands tied behind her back, she didn't have a lot to use besides her body and legs and Kassandra had loved to show her how to kick.

Hope did her best round house kick, managing to hit Sandra in the side of the head. When Sandra staggered back Hope followed her and shoved her back against the wall. When she heard her make a loud umph sound Hope thought she would take her chance and make a run for the door. If Gabriel was not here she might be able to make it outside and into the woods.

Hope ran out the door looking around. To the left, there appeared to be another room at the end of the hall but to the right, it looked like the hall opened into the living room. She sighed and chose to go right hoping that there was no one else in the house.

She found herself alone in the living room so she hurried to the front door and turned in order to use her hands, which were still tied behind her back. A crashing noise behind her let her know Sandra had managed to get back up so Hope hurried to finish twisting the handle while using her body to push it open. Nothing had sounded better to her than the squeak of the hinges as the door opened and her footfalls as she ran outside.

When the door pushed open she ran outside. Besides being surrounded by woods there was also a gravel road. Hope took off towards the woods knowing that the gravel road would be too easy to follow. She'd started to run when she felt a body hit her from behind.

Her hands still behind her back, she was unable to brace for the fall. The wind was knocked from her and it felt like she slid along the gravel face first. The weight of Sandra made it hard to breathe. She felt a hand slide into her hair then she got yanked back up onto her feet.

"I promised I wouldn't hurt you until after Warrick gets here," Sandra said as she began to try and drag her back to the house by her hair.

Hope tried to stand as Sandra pulled her. Half crawling, she followed along, wanting to pull back but Sandra's grip on her hair was so tight Hope thought for sure she would be bald when she let her go. Into the house, past the front room, Sandra pulled her into the bedroom before releasing her.

"I'm going to enjoy cutting you in front of Warrick. If I were you I'd be quiet because I'd hate for him to get here to find you already dead."

With that, Sandra slammed the door leaving Hope alone in the dark. She lay on the floor pulling her legs up as a tear slid down her cheek. The rope binding her hands felt just as tight as before and if Sandra was correct Warrick would be here soon. How was she going to help him?

Feeling herself start to give in to the feeling of despair she looked up to see something catch the light. The knife Sandra had dropped earlier was shining like a beacon. As she sat up she smiled thinking she would have a surprise for Sandra when she saw her.

24

Before leaving Sandra's, Kassandra had gone invisible and slipped into Jared's truck when Warrick opened the door. He was unable to smell or see her and found it oddly disturbing that he couldn't detect her. Warrick had heard about her gifts but had never experienced them before.

They told him when he opened any door to just give her enough time to slip past him. She made a small knocking sound once she had gotten out of the truck and into his house to let him know she was inside. Warrick paced back and forth, reaching out the best he could with his mind to his twin. *Where have you taken her Gabriel? You can't hide forever.*

Warrick whoever said I was hiding? I just wanted to make sure you came alone.

Warrick clenched his hands into a fist. His brother was close enough to hear him and respond. Was Hope? Why couldn't he feel them? *Where's my mate?*

He heard Gabriel make a tsking noise in reply. *Get in your truck and drive out of town, alone.*

Warrick made a point to unlock his truck from inside the house, opening the door before reaching back and turning off the lights. If anyone were watching him they wouldn't have realized he was giving someone enough time to slip past.

After he opened the door to his truck he made a point to drop his keys. Not sure if his brother was watching him or not, he gave her just enough time to crawl in before he slipped into the driver's seat. With everyone searching for Hope in the woods the town seemed oddly quiet. The few houses that he passed that had lights on all had a candle in the window. A silent show of support for Hope.

As he drove in silence he knew that if his brother were close he would notice him talking to someone, so he thought about Hope. She had quickly won over both packs. Her smile lit up every room she walked into and when he heard her laugh he often found himself smiling. She was his world and if his brother did anything to hurt her...

I can feel your anger brother. Didn't father say alphas should be able to control their feelings?

Warrick growled low. *You keep trying to steal what isn't yours baby brother. Time someone teaches you what happens to wolves who try to take things that aren't theirs'.*

Gabriel laughed in response then saw a truck pull out in front of him. *Follow me big brother...winner takes all.*

Winner takes all. Warrick repeated knowing he would have no choice but to kill his brother. Gabriel had to know that there was no way the pack would take him back. He definitely would not be able to take over as alpha. Even if Gabriel killed him tonight, Damien and the dragons would rip him to shreds before they let black magic take over the packs again.

This was a fight between the two of them. Gabriel fighting for everything he thought he deserved, Warrick fighting to keep everything he loved. He loved her. Before, when Gabriel had him tied to the table and was torturing Warrick, it was to keep safe a little girl he knew was meant for him. Now, as a man, he followed his brother's truck, this time sacrificing himself for the woman he loved more than life itself.

"I love her," Warrick said out loud knowing Kassandra was sitting quietly next to him. "Whatever happens tonight I need her to know that I love her."

He felt something touch his arm and knew that it was Kassandra letting him know she understood why he said those words out loud. If his brother killed him she would make sure that Hope was okay and that she would know.

They drove for several hours until he turned down some highway. The road was small and they drove for several miles before finally turning off to drive up a gravel driveway. Warrick's wolf, close to the surface, felt like a pent up animal in his head. He couldn't feel or sense Hope at all but somehow seemed to know that she would be there.

The truck in front of him parked and he parked next to it leaving the door open as he did. Kassandra's phone had GPS and he knew that Damien would not be far behind. "Let her go Gabriel, this fight is between you and me."

Gabriel came out from behind the truck, a smile on his face. If you took away the scars on Warrick the two of them would be the spitting image of each other. Amazing how one could look at a mirage of themselves and feel so much hate and anger.

"You really think you could take me? You couldn't all those years ago."

"Coming up behind me while I pulled their mother from the fire doesn't exactly count as a fair fight," Warrick said as he began to circle his brother. "You were a coward then and you're one now."

Warrick watched as Gabriel growled, his teeth lengthening and Warrick responded in kind. His wolf itching to come out. The two of them circling each other. Warrick was torn between fighting with his brother and running into the house to find Hope. He had to have faith that Kassandra would go into the house and find Hope. He knew that the best way to keep her safe was to deal with the problem in front of him.

The two of them lunged at each other shifting in the air. Warrick was born alpha so he shifted faster. His wolf was also bigger and when the two of them hit each other in the air Warrick realized exactly how much of an advantage that gave him. Even with a leg that hadn't healed perfectly he still had the upper hand.

Warrick could feel the impact of them hitting each other throughout his body. Gabriel hit the ground first Warrick landing on his feet next to him. He snapped at his brother, missing him as his brother rolled away.

The two of them lunged at each other again. This time Gabriel must have realized size was not going to be to his advantage and aimed lower on his chest, sinking his teeth into the muscle right above the shoulder. Warrick let out a howl of pain as he dropped his legs hard on his brother's chest, pulling his head and trying to break the hold.

Hope twisted her wrist almost painfully as she used the knife that Sandra had to cut the binds of her rope. When she heard two vehicles pull up she fought the urge to go and look and instead focused on the ties that bound her. As the binds on her wrist started to pull apart she heard someone walking to the door.

She worked the knife faster almost jumping when the door slammed opened and Sandra walked in. "Your mate is here," she started to say but then she narrowed her eyes as if she sensed something was different.

With one last yank of the knife Hope felt the rope give and she smiled while she began to walk closer to the front door. "What's wrong Sandra? Did you forget something?"

Hope watched as it suddenly dawned on Sandra that she had left her knife in the room earlier. That moment was enough to give Hope the advantage so she reached up to remove the necklace around her neck that had been causing the disconnect from her wolf and her pack.

Sandra lunged at her, the room too small for them to shift. Hope let out her wolf just enough to feel her claws and teeth lengthen, so she landed a hook to Sandra's left cheek. It was more satisfying than it should be to see her head swing back, but unfortunately, she didn't have time to enjoy it.

Based on how quickly Sandra recovered Hope figured this must not have been the first time she had been punched in the face. Sandra tried to land a cross that Hope managed to duck as she tried to land a punch of her own. When Hope missed, she lost her balance just enough for Sandra to get the advantage and land a knee to her stomach knocking the wind out of Hope.

Hope lost her footing and took a step backward when Sandra landed a glancing blow to her jaw. Hope was holding the knife in her left hand and switched it over to the right. When Sandra went to punch her again Hope raised the knife and managed to slice Sandra's arm, causing her to pull back with a hiss.

"Let me go Sandra. It's over," Hope said as she looked for an opening. "Warrick's here which means my brother won't be far behind. Run now and get away."

Sandra let out a laugh that sounded almost panicked. "You ruined my life and I'm going to take yours."

With that Sandra lunged for her and Hope's training kicked in. She stabbed Sandra in the stomach. It felt nothing like when she and Kassandra played with wooden swords. Instead she felt the blade sink in and felt horrified as she realized what she had just done.

Sandra let out a small gasp, as she looked down at the knife in her lower stomach. Hope took a step back not sure what to do. When Sandra reached down to take the knife out of her stomach Kassandra materialized from nowhere.

"If you pull that out you will bleed to death. Your body won't be able to heal fast enough to stop the bleeding," Kassandra said as she stepped into the room. "You have two choices, pull it out and bleed to death or apply pressure and live for a little while. At least until either Warrick kills Gabriel or Damien gets here."

Hope watched in horror as Sandra pulled out the knife and her shirt darkened from the blood. Sandra tried to lunge at her with the knife above her head. Unable to move, Hope watched as Sandra stumbled and fell to the ground. When she bent down to check her pulse Kassandra stopped her by putting her hand on her arm. "There's nothing we can do for her. She made her choice."

Hope nodded in understanding as the sound of two wolves outside caught her attention. "Warrick," she said, as she nearly ran into Kassandra in her rush to go the door. "I need to help him."

"Hope, if you go out there you'll distract him" Kassandra said putting her hand on the living room door stopping her from opening it. "Damien is on the way but as alpha to his pack, you need to let him handle his brother."

She understood what Kassandra meant. As alpha it was Warrick's job to protect his pack, as her mate it was his job to keep her safe. Gabriel had also kept him locked away and had tortured him for years. This was a fight he needed to finish.

25

Warrick felt his brother's teeth nip into his hind leg before he was able to pull it way. Warrick felt Hope suddenly and knew she was in the house. That moment of distraction was enough to let his brother bite him hard just above his bad knee. He almost gave up when he felt a sense of relief and worry for him.

An image of Hope in their bed, her blonde hair across the pillow as she smiled at him, gave him the desire to win this fight. Gabriel was no longer going to stand between him and the life he'd dreamed about.

Warrick mentally linked with Gabriel. *I feel my mate. You lost.*

He heard his brother growl in response. *What makes you think you can win?*

I have everything to live for he said before lunging at his brother. The two of them hitting chest to chest when the sound of vehicles coming up the driveway distracted Gabriel just enough for him to turn his head. That small opening was all Warrick needed to sink his teeth into his brother's neck. As he sunk his teeth past the fur and into his flesh Warrick could taste the blood on his tongue letting him know he had latched on.

Gabriel tried to twist his neck causing Warrick's teeth to sink in deeper. The more Gabriel twisted under him the tighter Warrick's grip became. When Gabriel tried to move again Warrick twisted his head tearing the flesh a bit. When his brother finally whimpered, putting his head down farther in a sign of submission, he debated for a moment before finally releasing him. His brother shifted first lying down, his neck exposed and Warrick could see the depth of his bite mark. If his wolf had bitten a man and not a wolf, he would be dead.

Warrick heard the door open to the house and saw Hope standing there. Turning from Gabriel he ran toward Hope only to have her jump into his arms. As he held her tight all those words of love stuck in his throat.

A growl from behind Warrick caused him to release Hope pushing her behind him. As he turned to see Gabriel lunging with his teeth bared. Before he could react he heard the loud bang of a gun going off. Warrick watched as his brother fell to the ground before him. Damien stood behind Gabriel with a gun in his hand.

"I should've done that the first time," Damien said, looking at the two of them. "Do me a favor and put some pants on I don't need my wife seeing your naked ass."

Warrick blushed a bit looking past Hope toward Kassandra in the doorway. With a smirk on her face and a raised eyebrow, she just shrugged her shoulders. "He's a little possessive. There should be some pants in the back of the vehicle that should fit you."

A glance at Hope showed she had a slight blush on her cheeks from all the attention and he kissed her hard on the lips before turning to grab the pants. As he turned he saw his brother laying naked on the ground a hole in his back where his heart was. If anyone but Damien would have shot him Warrick would believe that the wound would heal but he knew that the bullet was full of liquid silver and a type of poison Aithne had found that was fatal to wolves.

There was a sense of loss for his brother. When they were kids he would have never imagined that this would have ever happened. A memory of them as kids playing tag in the yard, laughing and having fun. The feel of Hope's hand on his back brought him back to the present. Shaking it off he carefully walked around his brother's body to go to the SUV and grab a pair of pants from the back.

He felt Damien behind him before he turned around. Warrick wasn't surprised to see Damien looking at him. "I'm sorry I killed your brother."

Warrick thought about what to say. "My brother killed your father, kidnapped your sister, and probably would've killed her. You did what you had to."

"He was still your brother," Damien said, giving him a look that said he understood the mixed emotions he was currently feeling.

Before he could think of anything to say he saw Hope walking toward him. Her lip was cut, her eye was mostly swollen, and he noticed that her hand was shaking as she pushed the hair back from her face. "Gabriel gave up the right to be called my brother the first time he put her in danger."

Damien nodded and he patted him on his arm as he walked by. He stood in front of Hope and gently cupped her cheek forcing her to look at him. "Where's Sandra?"

Hope started to open her mouth to tell him when she suddenly burst into tears. He pulled her close and saw Kassandra. She gave a shake of her head letting him know that Sandra was no longer a threat. Warrick bent down picking Hope up in his arms. When he started to walk back to his vehicle he noticed Viktor and Chase for the first time. They had pulled in behind Damien and he saw that they were now talking as they watched him.

Warrick carried Hope to the truck and opened the door with one hand. When he put her in he waited for her to release him before he stepped back. Hope gave him a shaky smile letting him know she was okay.

He walked around to the driver's side door giving the guys a wave before he got in and drove off. As shifters, they would understand his need to be alone with his mate. Warrick drove back to their home.

After a few minutes he felt Hope put her head on his shoulder.

"I killed her," she whispered quietly.

Warrick took her hand and squeezed it, "I'm sorry you had to do that. Sandra made her choice when she decided to follow my brother."

He could feel her nod on his shoulder and he thought about what to say. "I should have been the one to kill Gabriel."

He felt Hope's eyes on him and he turned to glance at her. "No, you shouldn't have. You did right by sparing his life."

Warrick felt his throat constrict a bit. They drove the rest of the way home in silence. Hope kept her head on his shoulder. That simple touch soothing him. When they pulled up to the house Hope started to open the door.

He got out quickly, walked around, and picked her up before she could close the passenger's door. Hope opened the front door for him and he took the stairs to their bedroom two at a time. She smelled of his brother and Sandra, he needed to rid her of that.

Warrick carried her to the bathroom and set her down on her feet. He bent down and undid her boots before he slid them off her feet, one at a time. Since he was already on his knees, he undid her pants, the sound of the zipper barely louder than her breathing. As he hooked his fingers into the top of her jeans, he looked up at her, meeting her amber eyes, and rolled her pants down her legs.

Hope didn't say anything as she reached down and cupped his cheek. The look in her beautiful eyes was inviting and she seemed to understand his need to remove the scent from her body. When he stood up he grabbed the bottom of her shirt and pulled it up and over her head in one move, tossing it on top of the discarded jeans.

"Don't move," he commanded before he gave her one hard quick kiss.

He left her long enough to turn on the shower and remove his clothes. After he was as naked as Hope, he tested the water to make sure it was warm enough. Warrick offered his hand to Hope and when she slid her delicate hand into his, he pulled her toward him.

When they both were in the shower he watched as she tilted her head up and let the water massage her scalp. The slight arch caused her breasts to push up and toward him. Too much temptation for him to resist so he reached up and cupped her breasts, rolling them between his fingers.

"I thought I'd lost you," he said when she let out a small sigh.

26

Hope reached out and cupped his cheek. The look on Warrick's face told her so much more than words ever could. She would like to have believed she wasn't vain enough to need the words but eventually she would. For now she could live with the knowledge that he cared about her.

"I knew you'd come for me." Hope smiled when he stepped closer to her looking down with a hunger in his eyes that made her core contract in need. "You've always been my knight in shining armor, even if I didn't know it."

She watched as a blush spread on Warrick's cheek. She knew he felt uncomfortable and she bit her lip to keep from laughing. Instead she gave in to the urge and slid her hand around his neck to pull him down to her and finally said the words that she thought she might never have a chance to say, "I love you Warrick."

Those words seemed to unleash something in him and he picked her up pinning her to the shower wall. She wrapped her legs around his waist as he lowered her onto his thick hard cock. Her body wasn't totally ready for him and she let out a small gasp that he muffled with a hard kiss.

There was something sexy about being pinned against the tile shower wall and the feel of the water hitting her naked flesh. Warrick held still inside her until she nipped at his neck, a demanding growl escaping her. His chuckle caused his chest to rub against her sensitive flesh and she let out a happy sigh when he finally started to move inside her.

Warrick thrust hard and she moaned using the muscles in her legs to raise and lower herself. Hope whimpered as he pulled out slowly, and let out a moan of pleasure when he thrust hard into her. With her nails on his shoulders, she felt her fingers curl and knew her nails were digging slightly into his flesh. When he thrust in again she panted, "Oh god Warrick, I love you."

He grunted again and began to thrust harder into her. At this angle, every time he pumped into her she felt him brush her clit, which only enhanced her pleasure. When he picked up the pace she leaned back against the wall and cupped his cheek forcing him to look at her. He still hadn't said anything since she'd said I love you and was starting to feel a little vulnerable.

Hope moved her hand to the wall to get better leverage, then captured his mouth with a rough kiss. His tongue thrusting into her mouth at the same tempo as his cock.

When she moaned, he captured it with another kiss and she felt her legs tighten around him. She needed him to move faster and showed him with her body. Her free hand slid into his hair, her nails digging slightly into his scalp. As her legs tightened around his waist she pulled him deeper and when he thrust his tongue back into her mouth she sucked on it.

A small giggle almost escaped her when she heard his growl. He then began to thrust faster, harder into her while his other hand slid up her side to tease her breast. Her nipples were so hard she was sure there was an imprint on his chest. When he began to tease her nipple she let out a small gasp breaking the kiss as her head fell back. Small currents of pleasure ran from her breast to the spot where their bodies were joined, showing how her body was connected and all centered on her release.

She felt Warrick begin to lick and kiss along her jaw and neck, his teeth teasing the column of her neck. She shuddered as he got close to his mating mark and continued to thrust. His breath burned hot against her flesh.

When she felt his breath right above where he left his mark she heard him demand in a rough, thick, unrecognizable voice, "Say it again."

The need echoed her own and she turned her head to slide her teeth down the column of his neck. When her teeth scraped over her mark on him she felt her canines lengthen and she whispered, "I love you Warrick."

The second those words had left her mouth she sunk her teeth into his flesh, into the mating mark and felt his growl as it echoed off the walls in the shower. His thrusts picking up and the shared pleasure from him inside her joined their bodies as they again marked each other as mates. It was all too much and she screamed against his neck as she felt herself go over.

Hope distantly heard his grunt. He thrust hard into her, her body tightening in response, as he went over with her. When they both started to come down she smiled against his neck her tongue coming out and licking where she'd bitten. She felt his tongue licking his bite mark and she smiled against his neck feeling that list twitch of his cock still deep inside her.

When she pulled back to look at him, she cupped his cheek and kissed him tenderly, their tongues dueling slowly this time and she could taste her blood on his lips. When he slipped from her core she let out a small whimper, missing the connection before slowly sliding her legs down his thighs.

They stayed that way for a few minutes, exchanging a few light kisses as the water continued to caress their bodies. After a bit he turned her so she was back under the water. She watched as he put shampoo in his hands, rubbing them together he moved in behind her and started to wash her hair. Massaging her scalp gently with his hands she moaned. When he was done she felt him start to rinse her hair.

Hope let him continue and watched as he put a decent amount of conditioner in his hand. Warrick slid it into her hair. She stopped him from rinsing it right away and shook her head, "I let it sit in my hair for a bit while I..."

When she blushed he smiled, kissing her tenderly. "Let me take care of you tonight."

She nodded, her eyes on him as he soaped up his hands. Warrick started with her back, massaging her muscles before going lower and massaging her backside. A moan escaped her but before she could enjoy it too much he lowered himself to his knees and massaged the back of her thighs. When Warrick finished, he tapped her leg telling her to turn around and she saw him grab the soap again.

This time he started at her feet, working her calf muscles before sliding up to her thighs. Higher and higher he went until she felt his fingers slide between her folds. Her lips parted as she let out a sigh and he cleaned her sensitive flesh.

"Warrick," she said his name on a sigh.

He stood up and continued his slow path washing her stomach moving up to gently clean her breasts while massaging them, before sliding down her arms, massaging every muscle down to her fingers. He then angled her back in the direction of the water to rinse her hair.

She felt treasured. The touch of his hand on her skin, the way he gently caressed her body. When he was finished washing her she watched as he quickly washed himself. Done in a fraction of the time it took him to wash her, she couldn't help but smile.

The water dried off and he patted her skin before simply wrapping the towel around himself. A small gasp of surprise left her when he picked her up again and carried her to the bed. "I can walk you know," she said as he laid her in the middle of the bed.

"I know," he said as he tucked her in.

Hope watched him walk back to the bathroom. She could see his shadow as he dried himself off. When he walked back out of the bathroom she couldn't help but admire his form. The scars on his body and face added a hint of mystery to his rugged handsomeness.

Warrick lay next to her in the bed and pulled her close. She heard his heart beating, listened to the sound of his breathing. He didn't say a word, just held her tight to his chest. After a few minutes she could feel him start to fall asleep. She knew enough about adrenaline to know that soon she would be joining him. A yawn escaped her and she nuzzled his chest giving in to the urge to close her eyes and let sleep claim her.

27

Warrick worked with Aithne to try and piece together where his brother had been. Their ultimate goal was to see if they could find where his brother hid the pack's money and find out more about the witches that had taken Hope and Damien's mother.

While Warrick did that, Hope and Kassandra had found a box of papers and receipts. Both of them spent their days trying to see what they could learn. That left Damien who spent most of his days with Chase putting the extra guards to work finishing up the town.

The morning after Hope was taken they woke up to find the house surrounded by their pack members all wanting to make sure Hope was okay. Some asked about Warrick but they lavished their attention on her. That made him smile, he remember his father ran the pack but his mother held it together with love and grace. Hope, in a few short months had won over the hearts of their people just like his mother had.

"Your brother loved his GPS," Aithne said looking up at him. "He thought he'd erased his history but he obviously didn't know much about computers."

Warrick grinned at that. "Nice to know I'm not the only person who doesn't know much about those things."

"To be fair, he definitely knows more than you do. But not nearly as much as I do," Aithne said with a hint of humor to her voice.

"You know you don't act much like a queen," Warrick said, leaning back in his chair.

Aithne laughed at that, pushing her long red hair behind her ear. She was wearing a plain green t-shirt that brought out the color in her eyes and a pair of faded blue jeans that looked like they had seen better days. Most of her hair was tied back in a braid but a few of the strands had escaped, framing her face.

"I think I should say thank you, but I'm not sure if you meant that as a compliment," Aithne said. She leaned back in the chair to look at him. "To be fair you don't look like what I picture when I think of an alpha wolf."

Warrick nodded with a casual shrug. Something in his reaction must have caught her attention because she instantly frowned. "Not for what you're thinking, Warrick. You're here with me going over the few belongings we could find. Back in my day, leaders used to sit around and watch others work. Claiming what others did as their own while they sat on a gilded thrown."

"Thank you," Warrick replied giving her a smile that said he understood. "I also forget you look amazing for how old you are."

That made her laugh and she picked up what looked to be some kind of ball and threw at him. She missed him by enough that he knew that it was on purpose. "You're in rare form today. But if you can be nice I'll tell you what I found."

Warrick couldn't stop smiling as he walked over to see what she was looking at. On the phone she held in her hand was a list of addresses she had pinpointed on the map on the computer. There were several plots between the cabin where they'd found him and West Virginia where the pack was previously located.

"There. This spot right here in Kentucky he seemed to frequent a lot. When I pulled up a satellite picture all I can seem to find is this cabin surrounded by woods. Not much else."

When Aithne showed him the image, Warrick found himself again humbled by all the things he had missed. He never imagined this would be possible. The cabin was in a clearing in the woods. Even from this angle he could see it was large.

"Is it me or is that cabin large?" Warrick asked.

Aithne nodded. "It is pretty big for a cabin. It's also on twenty-five acres. I looked it up and it's owned by several shell corporations. It is going to take a few weeks to find out if he owns it or not."

"What is something like this worth?" Warrick asked curious.

"The cabin alone is probably worth about a million dollars. The land is probably worth several million."

Warrick let out a small whistle. That could be all the packs money right there if it belonged to his brother. What would that mean if it turned out his brother had taken all their money and bought that? Would it be possible for them to get it back? Could he just sell it?

He let out a sigh rubbing the back of his neck. Aithne looked over her shoulder at him. A look of understanding crossed her face, "We'll figure it out. If it turns out your brother owns this place, good thing you two are twins. Go home. Kiss Hope. We will figure out the answers later."

"That sounds like a great idea."

He thanked her again before leaving, excited to get back home to his mate. On the drive home he wondered what else they would find at the ranch. If his brother was there a lot, there had to be a reason. Warrick was excited to get home and tell Hope what they had learned. She had texted him earlier and said she was home but she didn't mention finding anything so he knew she could use the good news.

HOPE HEARD WARRICK PULL UP. She smiled as she checked on the chicken in the oven. Every night he kissed her senseless, making love to her as he asked her to tell him she loved him. He never said it back, instead he made love to her body. Worshipped her with kisses and didn't stop making love to her until she was so satisfied the idea of moving made her tired.

The front door opened and she listened as he walked down the hall to the kitchen.

"How did it go with Kassandra?" Warrick asked as he gave her a kiss.

"Your brother seemed to have kept every receipt he ever got, for no particular reason. He also paid a lot in cash so we haven't been able to find a credit card for Kassandra to track down," Hope said. He heard the pout in her voice.

"Aithne was able to pull up his history on his GPS," Warrick told her as he started to get the plates down from the cabinets.

"Oh?" she asked curious.

"There's a cabin he kept going back to in Kentucky. She says it's on twenty-five acres and between the land and the house might be worth a few million dollars."

Hope stopped what she was doing and looked at him. "Few million..." she started to ask when he nodded. "Wow, is it his?" she asked, curious if that was where all the packs money went.

"Aithne says it is owned by several shell companies and it will take a bit for her to sort it out." She could feel Warrick's eyes on her as she took all the food out of the oven. They made their plates. The two of them talking about their day.

Hope loved how he constantly touched her. When they were done, he cleaned up and went upstairs where the two curled up in bed and made love until she couldn't move. Despite the fact that he constantly showed her that he cared for her, the longer he went without saying *I love you* the more she began to doubt that he did.

The moment Hope fell asleep she knew something was off. She was standing outside a door. Her hand came up to open it and she paused. Whatever was on the other side was going to change her life. The scent of roses hung in the air that reminded her of her mother and she felt an invisible hand touch her back. Even though she had very few memories of her mother the smell of roses always made her think of her.

With a deep breath, she grabbed the handle and opened the door. As she stood in the open doorway she could smell Warrick and the coppery smell of blood, a lot of blood. It smelled worse than the room they had found him in.

"Warrick," she whispered. As she took a step into the room, the door she stepped through disappeared, leaving her no choice but to go forward.

There was no answer, just an eerie silence that made her skin crawl. As she walked farther into the room she saw Warrick hanging by his arms. He had fresh cuts on his body and there was a big bowl on the ground. It had been positioned to collect his blood.

Hope reached out and her hand slid right through him.

"Hope," she heard him whisper before he groaned and opened his eyes. She wondered at first if he was able to sense her until she realized he was dreaming.

A loud bang from the opposite side of the room made her jump. Gabriel stumbled in drunk. "Still dreaming of your mate, Big Brother," Gabriel said. She wrinkled her nose when she smelled the alcohol on him. "She deserves better than someone like you. You couldn't save our parents. You helped us kidnap her mother. If you think you have it bad you should see what they've been doing to her mother. Yet here you hang, providing the blood to keep her people tied to me."

Hope felt her eyes tear up at his words. The idea that her mother had been tortured just like Warrick made her sick to her stomach. Gabriel walked over with a blade he grabbed from the table and sliced along Warrick side. "Let her mother go," Warrick said.

"Forever the hero," Gabriel said as he twisted the knife a bit into his side. "Holding onto the idea that if you do enough, your mate will love you back. You're broken, beaten, and you only live now because you begged me to let the witches use your blood to bind everyone and not Hope. She would never love a guy like you."

Hope couldn't stop the tears from sliding down her cheeks. His words so cruel she couldn't imagine anyone having to listen to that for fifty years. The torture, the cruel words, constantly being told how no one could possibly love him. Hope's heart broke for Warrick.

28

Hope awoke with a new understanding of what Warrick went through. Tears were still streaming down her face when she awoke. She wiped the tears from her eyes, smiling when she felt him roll over and pull her close as if sensing she needed his comfort. How could someone have gone through so much and still be so thoughtful?

Being held by him calmed her down, recalling her to the present. His brother was dead otherwise Hope would kill him herself. Too bad she couldn't kill him twice. As she drifted back to sleep she realized that she would need to find a way to show him that he was worthy of her love.

Over the next few days Kassandra worked with Aithne trying to figure out who owned the cabin in Kentucky. Since they didn't have much to do, she and Warrick started to make their rounds with the pack members. Damien was constructing a new gym for the kids and told her it was her job to represent him to help make the decisions.

The problems the people came to them with were small disputes between neighbors and advice on what to do to move forward. As they walked around the town talking to different pack members she watched Warrick listen intently to their problems. When he gave them advice or a solution the people hung on his every word. She doubted he knew how much he meant to them.

After making their rounds Hope laced her fingers with his. "They love you, you know."

Warrick looked over and she followed his gaze to see a few kids watching them from behind the house. "They're scared of me."

Hope smiled at the kids waving at them, they giggled and ran off. "I don't think they're scared of you. Just curious."

Warrick shook his head and she realized that he was really bothered by it. She picked up his hand and brought it to her lips kissing it. "You're their alpha. Trust me they're in awe of you. I remember the kids used to watch my father the same way."

When she turned to look at him she noticed he was frowning. The walk back to the house was quiet, both of them lost in their own thoughts. When they got inside she ordered pizza. Not the romantic dinner she had planned but it would work in a pinch.

After dinner Warrick left to go help Damien finish working on the house next door. Damien was eager to start his family with Kassandra and wanted their house to be perfect. Hope touched her stomach smiling. She'd told Damien that morning she thought she would get pregnant before Kassandra. Damien had laughed, both agreeing to a small bet. If she got pregnant first Damien would pay for her sunroom, if Kassandra got pregnant first, Hope would paint a mural on the baby's wall. Both of them knew, regardless who won, that she would do that for him.

After cleaning the house she took a quick shower, put on a small white baby doll nightie, and decided to read in bed while she waited for Warrick. When he finally got home it was close to midnight. Warrick gave her a kiss and she smiled. "Take a shower. You smell."

Warrick laughed, kissing her again and headed into the bathroom. When she heard the water running she got out and lit several candles around the bed. When everything was lit she laid on top the blankets adjusting the nightie, hoping she looked sexy.

The water stopped and she held her breath as she waited for him. When he stepped from the bathroom, a towel around his waist, she saw him pause when he looked at her. A blush spread across her cheeks when his eyes roamed her body.

"You look like a siren," he whispered before finally walking over to the bed.

Hope got onto her knees, reaching to the side of the bed she undid his towel and tossed it aside. When he gave her a look she smiled and pulled him down on the bed. Warrick seemed to know to follow her lead and laid in the middle of the bed looking up at her.

She bit her lip looking down at him. Her eyes scanning his body starting at his feet where she saw the scar around his knee. Going up his legs she saw a few more scars and scratches. She blushed when she noticed his cock had started to harden. She continued to look up his body, making note of every scar until she got to his face. That was where the biggest scar he had was and she wondered how much hatred his brother Gabriel would have had to have to do that to his mirror image. The scar was still noticeable but no longer drew your attention like before.

"You are so very sexy," Hope whispered as she went to lie on her side next to him. She propped herself up on an elbow and gently ran her hand across his stomach. Hope bent her head down and kissed his stomach, running her tongue along a scar that ran along his side.

Her fingers gently traced the muscles and every time she found a new scar she kissed it. The longer ones she traced with her tongue. Her fingers traced the side where she saw him get stabbed in her dream. She was surprised when she didn't find a scar. Despite not seeing anything she knew he was stabbed there and licked up his side anyway. When she got to his face she gently peppered the scars on his face with kisses.

Warrick grabbed her hips and moved her so she was straddling him. He slid his hands under the bottom of the nightie and gripped her ass. Hope leaned down at him cupping his cheek as she eyes met his.

"I love you Warrick. I know you probably don't believe me but I do love you and when I look at you I can't believe how lucky I am to have you as my mate. I don't expect you to love me yet, but one day I hope to hear those words from you. Until then I'll tell you over and over again and show you that whatever horrible things your brother told you were untrue."

Before she could finish her speech, Warrick rolled her over onto her back. His hips settling between her thighs. When she looked up she saw a fierce look in his eyes. He rolled his hips and she moaned, the thin material of the matching thong did nothing to stop her from feeling how hard and ready he was.

"My beautiful Hope. How could you possibly think I don't love you," Warrick said bending down to nuzzle her neck. "Whenever I thought about giving up, it was your memory that kept me from giving in to the darkness. You're my Hope, the love of my life and I'm so sorry you ever felt like you needed to earn my love."

As he whispered those sweet words into her ear, she felt his hands sliding under the silky material of the baby doll dress. When he finally reached her breasts she moaned, her back arching up trying to press her breast deeper into his hand.

She felt his lips curve in a smile. "I used to dream about making love to you. How your body would respond to my touch. Hearing you scream my name as you fell apart in my arms."

Warrick dipped his head and she gasped when she felt his tongue flicking over the material. When he pulled back she felt the material slide up and over her head. This time he bent down and sucked her nipple into his mouth. Her back arched up and off the bed as he teased one breast with his mouth and the other he massaged with his hand.

He alternated between them; one then the other. When he pulled back and looked up at her she reached down and cupped his cheek. "Tell me again you love me." Hope asked him.

"I love you Hope," he said, kissing her hand.

He adjusted his hips and she felt his cock press against her entrance. Hope wrapped her legs around him and tilted her hips. When she finally felt him start to slip inside her, she moaned, "I love you, Warrick."

This time they made love slowly. Hope touched him everywhere she could, running her hands along his back before gripping his firm ass. Warrick kissed along her neck while he teased her breast with his hand, sending small shivers down to her core with every tug.

"I love you –– I love you," Hope panted, loving how every time she got the words out he responded to her. She wanted to drag out this pleasure forever but when he nipped at her pulse she gave into the urge and growled. "Oh fuck, I love you," she said before she let her canines lengthen and bit into his mark as she let go.

Warrick's hips bucked harder and his shoulder muffled her scream of pleasure. He finally shouted, "I love you," before sinking his teeth into her flesh. The shared pleasure during the bite was so intense she went over again and was only distantly aware that he was joining her.

When the last wave of pleasure rolled through her, Hope released his neck and moaned softly, licking the place where she'd bitten. She felt him do the same as his cock slowly slipped from her. She felt Warrick get up and watched him go to the bathroom. He came back with a rag and gently cleaned her up. He put the washrag back in the bathroom before joining her in bed. Hope couldn't help but smile as he pulled her close. With his hand sliding up and down her back, she laid her head on his chest.

"I'm sorry Hope. I was a fool. I didn't realize how much I loved you until my brother took you. I wanted to tell you I loved you then, but I chickened out."

She lifted her head off his chest looking up at him. "I'll forgive you on one condition," she said with a smile. When he raised his eyebrow, she gave him an overly bright smile. "I have to get pregnant before Kassandra. We made a bet and I'm determined to win."

Warrick let out a loud laugh as he pulled her up and onto his chest. He gave her a big kiss and smiled against her lips. "Your wish is my command."

29

Warrick and Damien stood by the barbeque watching Hope and Kassandra. The pack kids had started to come over and play in their backyard over the last few weeks. The two of them, with the help of Aithne, had started teaching self-defense classes as a way to get to know the children and the families. Afterwards the kids would play in the yard. Kassandra had bought a bunch of guns that shot plastic darts and right now they were chasing the kids and shooting them.

"Hope looks happier than I've seen her in a very long time," Damien said to Warrick while taking a swig of his beer.

A scream of laughter caused Warrick to turn his head and look at the two girls. The kids had all joined forces and had started chasing Hope and Kassandra causing them to run away, both of them aiming wildly behind them as they ran.

"Your sister deserves it," Warrick replied smiling.

"So do you," Damien replied as he started to flip the steaks. "I never thanked you for what you did for us as kids."

Warrick felt his cheeks warm a bit and knew he was probably blushing. "You would've done the same thing. She was my mate and you're my brother."

Damien nodded and Warrick saw him glance at Kassandra. Warrick didn't feel like he'd done anything that any other wolf wouldn't do for his mate. The reality is that if they never came and rescued him he would have spent the rest of his life being tortured by his brother.

"Aithne thinks they'll have that cabin in Kentucky cleaned out soon and it already has buyers lined up," Warrick said as he watched the parents slowly start to show up to get their kids.

"It's going to take us months to go over the paperwork and files your brother kept," Damien said waving to a few of the parents.

Warrick nodded. When they first went to the house Warrick couldn't believe how much of their parent's stuff he had kept. Old pictures, his mother's jewelry. They even found some more journals that belonged to Hope and Damien's mother. Everything in the house was going in storage units to be sorted to see what other treasures they might find and if anything else belonged to the pack. Part of the money from the sale of the house would be used to payback Viktor and the rest to be divided among the pack members.

When the last of the kids got picked up, Damien grinned as he took the steaks off the grill. The girls went into the house to wash up and grab the sides so they could eat on the outside table. Everyone made a plate quickly. The steaks smelled delicious and the girls had made pasta salad. When everyone was seated Warrick looked at Hope who was grinning away. Warrick gave her a nod and she picked up her glass of lemonade.

"I have an announcement to make," Hope said, a big grin plastered on her face.

Damien smiled. "Really we have an announcement to make too."

The two of them looked at each other intently and Damien watched as Hope's eyes narrowed before both began speaking. "We're pregnant. I won the bet." They said in unison.

Warrick and Kassandra laughed at the look on both their faces. Both Hope and Damien frowned for a moment before Damien said, "Delivery date determines the winner?"

Kassandra shook her head. "No. I want my mural before the baby is born."

"And I want my sunroom." Hope said, making a face as she thought it over. "Why don't we compromise? I'll paint your mural and Warrick will help you build my sunroom."

"But I get to pick out the mural," Kassandra said as she gave Damien a look.

"Done," Hope agreed, laughing when her brother started to protest.

"Congratulations Kassandra," Warrick said getting up to give her a kiss on the cheek.

"To you too," Kassandra said getting up and hugging Hope.

Damien and Warrick gave each a pat on the back, which made Kassandra roll her eyes at them. "Don't be congratulating each other yet. Your job is done."

They both chuckled and Warrick took Hope's hand. She looked even more radiant now than she did before. Everyone got quiet when Hope looked at her brother. "You know what this means right?" she asked.

"Mom's letter said she will be with us before the first baby is born," Damien said.

Warrick could feel an array of emotions coming from both of them. Their mother had told them not to look for her. That she would be with them before the first of her grandbabies was born. They never thought that the two of them would both be having children at the same time.

ABOUT LEILANI LOVE

Leilani Love is a proud mother of two very active boys. She loves traveling to new places and meeting new people wherever she goes. Thus far, Leilani has visited Paris, DenBosch and Amsterdam and hopes to one-day return. On her next trip she hopes to be able to make stops in Scotland and Italy. Currently residing in Oregon, she has also lived in Hawaii, Florida, Alaska, Virginia, Texas, Washington and California. She loves to read books and has a passion for various genres. Her love affair with dragons began when she was young and she still dreams of having her own dragon and Black Panther. For now, she is content to write about them in her books.

You can follow her on her Facebook page at:
www.facebook.com/missleilanilove